POP-CULT®

PUBLISHING

Since 1977

nart@fastcheapandeasy.com

Fast, Cheap & Easy Graphics

Produced by Pop-Cult Publishing in cooperation with
Fast, Cheap & Easy Graphics

CONVENIENCE

by Jack Yaghubian

Convenience / Jack Yaghubian 1949—

First edition/revision 1.9

Other books by Jack Yaghubian: *the Dim Light bar guide Volume 1, Grunt's Minutia, the Dim Light bar guide Second Edition*

Available at City Lights Booksellers on the hypotenuse in North Beach, San Francisco.

Credits:

The jacket design and illustrations throughout were done by Fast, Cheap & Easy Graphics. The illustrations were done using photographs taken by the FC&EG staff, with the exceptions of several photos which were found on the web: pages 36, 39, 40, 48 (Mab sign only, photo of building was taken by FC&EG recently), 113. Several others were taken by: John Gullak (page 16), Hugh Brown (cover image and pages 46, 65 and 71), Michael Granros (pages 61, 74, 114,130, and 139), Barbara Wyeth (page 150) and one which was taken in a photo booth by Hollyce Fagerhaugh (page 52). Lastly, at my request, Joanna Lioce managed to write the word *convenience* on a scrap of paper which was used to produce the images on pages 10 and 188.

Acknowledgements:

Jessica Loos, who did two edits of this book halfway through production and one as we were nearing completion. Although the Pop-Cult editors overrode many of her suggestions for stylistic reasons, she did set us straight on a number of issues and helped tremendously in the completion of this project.

Earl 'The Pearl' Adkins who, when I told him I was thinking about writing a book about the underground club scene in San Francisco in the early 1980s, offered to serialize it in his paper the *Marina Times* if I did. With that encouragement I started on it, got sidetracked and *Convenience* was the result.

Dedicated to the human body, which is 60% water.

John Simon's Travels

1) The Rabbit Hole
2) Mystic Eye
3) Enrico's
4) Mabuhay Gardens
5) The Machine Shop Arcade
6) Vesuvio
7) Gulliver's
8) Saloon
9) Cafe Trieste
10) Ben's Poster Matt
11) Schlock Shop
12) S&S Market
13) Savoy Tivoli
14) Luther Blue's
15) Michaels
16) Sam Wo Resturant
17) Garden of Eden

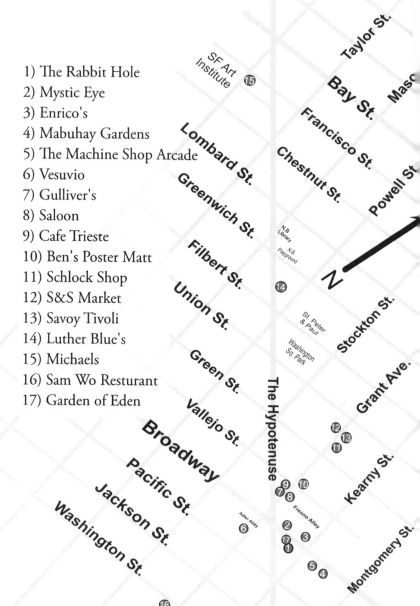

Preface

This project began in the fall of 2016 as a short story titled "Convenient." After reading the original draft of "Convenient," my editor, Jessica "The White Queen" Loos, said that she didn't know if it was a short story. I took that to mean I should expand on the idea, which I did. The initial expansion became what is now the epilogue, "The Detention Center." The original short story is now the prologue, "Convenient." As mentioned in the Credits section, Jessica also did three edits of the entire book. I should also mention that, never one to leave well enough alone, I made numerous changes after her last edit, so I take full responsibility for any abnormalities found herein.

The portion of this book that takes place in 1979 was written largely from memory, with some research where I found it necessary and with help from friends who were also around North Beach in those days. It helped that I still live in the neighborhood where the story takes place, because the buildings and some of the people are still here.

Most of it is accurate, with regard to people, places and the time frame of spring 1979, though I have taken liberties where it helped the story line. Most of the characters are based on real people, but some are a mishmash of several people I have known and others are totally made up. I'll leave to the reader to figure out which is which. The portion that takes place in the future is, of course, all conjecture.

Four years after I began, the short story has grown into the book *Convenience*. Another book I wrote, *Grunt's Minutia*, also began as a short story. What I have learned from this is, the next time I have an idea for a book, I will start by writing a short story.

~JY October 2020

P.S. Regardless of what the dedication page says, this book was written for the denizens of North Beach, past, present and future and for those who have a North Beach state of mind.

We choose to do this,
not because it is hard,
but because it is convenient.

San Francisco 2063

Prologue

ENIENT CONVENIENT
ENIENT CONVENIENT
CNIENT CONVENIENT
VENIENT CONVENIEN
VENIENT CONVENIEN
VENIENT CONVENIEN
WENIENT CONVENIEN
VENIENT CONVENIE
ONVENIENT CONVENIE
ONVENIENT CONVENIE
ONVENIENT CONVENI
ONVENIENT CONVENI
CONVENIENT CONVEN
CONVENIENT CONVER
CONVENIENT CONVE
CONVENIENT CONVER

Convenient

S O... MY NAME IS ALICE, ALTHOUGH HERE THEY CALL ME D3. Before they put me here my life was very convenient. I am single, so I lived in a pod. Though small, as pods tend to be, everything was tasteful, well designed and conveniently placed. When I went out I summoned a ride with a few taps on my device. While I was out my desires were satisfied and paid for with a few more taps. The places I frequented were new, safe and accommodating. The food I ate was of the highest quality and of the most recent trends in fine dining. I felt so smart, so successful, so sophisticated. Yes, my life was convenient.

This room is clean and my basic needs are met, however, this room is not convenient: There is a bed, a table and chair, and a toilet-sink-shower unit. Food is sent to me, in that dumbwaiter over there, three times a day. At least I think it is. There are no windows, no clock, and the lights are always on, so how could I know?

The walls are white, or at least they were. Now they are slowly turning gray. That is my fault. They gave me pencils and paper with which I am supposed to write a confession. I have no idea what I am supposed to confess, so I sit here alone, wondering what they want me to write.

I am sorry; as I was saying, the gray walls are my fault. As a way to mark time, after every third meal I write the word *convenient* on the wall with one of my pencils. It is sort of a hobby. I have been here a long time and I know that eventually I may fill all of the available wall space. I worry about that. Maybe I will figure out a way to reach the ceiling and that will give me more time and space.

Since I have been here I have had a lot of time to think. For instance, when did the word *convenient* become synonymous with sophistication and the good life? I have come to suspect it was intentional, perhaps a subliminal ad campaign. Maybe I should have questioned all the convenience I enjoyed. Maybe I should not mention that. Maybe that is why I am here. I must remember to include that in my confession.

So… I think it started with a conversation I had in a bar a couple of weeks or so before they put me here. The bar was called The Rabbit Hole. A guy I was dating at the time suggested we meet there, otherwise I never would have gone into such a place.

I was sitting at the bar waiting for my date when this old man in a hat with a little white beard sat on the bar stool next to mine. Soon we started a conversation during which he occasionally stopped to greet one of the bar's regulars. He had nicknames for them all; one he called The White Queen, another The Red Queen and another The Cheshire Cat. He introduced himself as Hatter, which I suspect is also a nickname.

At one point in our conversation marijuana was mentioned. Apparently it used to be illegal. In his opinion the reason it was legalized was to keep the population docile. He said that when this country was primarily a manufacturing nation at near full employment, tobacco was needed to dull the tedium and alcohol was needed to kill the physical and mental pain caused by repetitive, physical work. He said now that over thirty-percent of the population is permanently unemployed they need to be kept distracted and docile. He said if marijuana was not legal, cheap, and readily available the u-bees would become restless.

He had other crazy ideas as well. For instance, he said that voting was pointless because the corporations owned the government and they run it however they please.

At that point I had had enough of this guy and his forbidden speech. I was about to move to another place at the bar, when he referred to my device as a *telescreen*. That annoyed me, I loved my device, so I asked him what he meant by that. He said that is what devices were called in the book *1984* by George Orwell. The year 1984 was over fifty years before I was born, so I thought that a book from that date had little to do with me. I never read it and I told him so.

He told me that telescreens were spying devices placed in homes and offices or hidden behind two-way mirrors by The Thought Police. He said Orwell got that wrong because now people willingly carry them and pay for the privilege. He said Edward Snowdon made the same criticism from exile in Russia.

While I used my device to Google *Edward Snowdon*, Hatter had a fit over digital payments, which I also used all the time, I never carried cash. Who does? In fact the bar we were sitting in did not accept digital payments. I had to go to the ATM to get cash just to buy a drink. Can you imagine that? It is so inconvenient. Well, in his opinion digital payments were part of the corporate takeover of government. He said when cash was discontinued I would not be able to have a yard sale, a poker game, or loan a friend money without some corporate entity taking a cut and keeping a record of the transaction.

I pointed out that I never did any of those things and that I never paid extra to use digital payments. Then I added that I had nothing to hide, so they could keep all the records they wanted.

His answer was that the businesses pay the bank charges, then raise their prices to help defray the costs, so we all pay more. He said one of the reasons there are so few single location businesses anymore is that digital payments give the chain stores an additional advantage over single location businesses. He added that someday I might regret that they kept a record of all my digital transactions. Sitting here now, that thought makes a chill go up my spine.

I became weary of Hatter's depressing conversation and glanced around the bar, wondering what was taking my date so long. That was when he told me that the protagonist of *1984* was Winston Smith and that his job was to rewrite history so that it agreed with what The Ministry of Truth was saying. He said that eBooks make that much easier because it only takes a few key strokes to censor all copies on every device in the world.

From a college class on early 21st century history I remembered that Amazon did something like that; they sold a digital reprint of a book that they thought was in the public domain. They were issued a Cease & Desist by the lawyer who represented the copyright holder, so they just erased all existing copies they had sold and refunded the purchase price. And, if I remember correctly, the book was *1984*. It created quite an uproar. But of course that was in the old days, nobody would care now, they would just take the refund and move on.

Hatter eventually moved away to talk with another old man. Shortly after that my date arrived and said it was a mistake to suggest that we meet at The Rabbit Hole. He practically dragged me out of there. He did not even let me finish my drink. I never saw Hatter again, but our conversation stuck with me and as time passed I began to obsess over it.

Dinner and Drinks
Chapter 1

I WANDERED AIMLESSLY AND ALONE THROUGH DOWNTOWN San Francisco. Gleaming 21st century sky scrapers lined the streets, dwarfing the drab efforts of earlier times. The older buildings, though not so impressive for their height or glitz, did give one a sense of history and place, two things the newer ones lacked.

Occasionally I glanced at the shop windows I passed. There were a few real windows, but they were for shops with a security door that wouldn't open for unauthorized faces. Referred to as *convenience stores*, they were for serious and wealthy clients only, not browsers. Other than places where people consumed things, such as bars, cafes, and restaurants, the convenience stores were the only remaining brick and mortar shops in The City.

Most of the windows I passed were virtual shop windows. Sometime in the 2020s San Francisco passed a city ordinance that in legacy commercial districts, street level real estate had to have a facsimile of a shop window. The downtown was one of those districts.

I was wearing my spectaculars, so the items on display in the virtual windows were for my eyes only. Other people wearing their specs saw different items than I did. Occasionally I took my specs off when I grew tired of looking at things based on my shopping history. When I did, displayed in those same virtual windows were spinning holographic images of new and convenient products.

Unseen behind the virtual windows were office space, server farms, expedited delivery warehouses, vertical farms, and living space for a city with a population of almost two million residents. With nearly everything delivered to your door from warehouses outside of the city limits, plenty of additional mixed use real estate became available in The City during the 2020s as brick and mortar retail was ending.

As I wandered my specs notified me that my date, Sarah, was approaching in an auto-car. I was nervous because this would be our first in person meeting. I looked to the street and saw a white-car pull up to the curb. White-cars are a basic form of transportation, they are the cheapest and most popular auto-car. Sarah beckoned me from inside the small, two seat vehicle. I removed my specs and put them into my jacket pocket. As the auto-car door opened, she said, "Johnny Boy, get in!"

Though we had never met in person, we had been dating online for several months and had been having virtual sex for over a month. As I got into the auto-car my nostrils were assaulted by an offensive odor which I did my best to ignore. "I am sorry, it smells like someone peed in this white-car," Sarah commented, looking and sounding embarrassed.

"All white-cars smell like this," was my consoling reply. *Or of something much worse*, I thought.

After an awkward first hug in the cramped confines of the auto-car, Sarah asked, "Where would you like to eat, Johnny Boy?"

I replied that I wasn't a picky eater and that anywhere would be fine with me. She tapped her device and the auto-car lurched forward, then made a right turn at the next corner.

After a short trip down Market Street we turned right onto Cyril Magnin Street, then pulled up to the curb. As we got out Sarah waved her hand in front of her face, as if to rid herself of the offending odor. "People are such animals," she said. With that off her chest, her comments became upbeat, "This place has the best spare ribs. You said you had no food preferences."

"No, I will eat pretty much anything," I replied, as we crossed the street. I considered the restaurant we were about to enter. It was a typical downtown place that catered to tourists. Large signage was splashed across the front of the building that read, The Barbary Bistro. The sign was set in an Old West typeface that was embellished with flashing red lights. In addition to the sign, a depiction of a nineteenth century gold miner was painted on the building above the entrance. The image included the restaurant's logo which was based on a pick ax and a miner's pan. Below the logo, painted in small type, was Autoteria Inc. Autoteria is the name of a chain of inexpensive, automated restaurants of which The Barbary Bistro was one.

"I know, I know," Sarah said defensively, reading the expression on my face. "But the tourists turn their noses up at soylent, so this place serves real meat. Real meat, Johnny Boy!"

The sliding doors opened at our approach, then slid closed behind us as we entered a large room that was very clean, brightly lit and almost empty. We were immediately confronted by the lone employee; a man dressed in a garish costume that was a mishmash of blue jeans, a polo shirt, green rubber rain boots, and a yellow hard hat. Around his waist he wore a thick, brown belt with a huge metal buckle that had the logo of the restaurant incorporated into its design. "Welcome to The Barbary Bistro," he greeted us in a forced cheery tone of voice. I smiled at him and nodded.

Then I took a moment to consider the decor, which consisted of reproductions of paraphernalia from the 19th century gold rush era, printed with a 3-D printer and then affixed to the walls. There were also 2-D painted design elements on the walls, interspersed between the 3-D imagery. These included several old fashioned farm vistas populated by frolicking pigs and chickens. Pork and chicken were the only kinds of meat one was likely to encounter in a place like The Barbary Bistro.

But I also noticed, with some initial confusion, that there were a number of basic happy face emoji, painted in gaudy colors, among the farm images. More disturbing, the word *enjoy* was painted just below each one, using Gill sans, a basic, old fashioned typeface. *Not a very adventurous choice of typeface. That's what you get when you use a design algorithm*, I thought with amusement. I'm an interior designer, so such things interest me.

I'd never been in this particular restaurant, but I had been in a few of Autoteria's other operations. They tried to make each one look different by choosing a different theme, but since they were all decorated by an algorithm they all ended up looking more or less the same. The design algorithms were improving, but in the better places they still used human designers. In my workspace the joke was that we were all one new algorithm away from u-beeism. *U-bee* is short for the recipients of Universal Basic Income. They are redundant, unemployable people that the corporations pay not to work.

I quickly grew bored with the trite, computer generated decor and glanced at Sarah. She was a tall, healthy female with a pretty face who wore her blond hair cut short. Her taste in clothes was simple: a white shirt, tan pants, white canvas shoes and if she was wearing make-up, it wasn't noticeable. I found her to be very attractive, which isn't always the case when you meet an online date in person.

I've always found that first in person dates are awkward. Sarah buried her face in her device as soon as we entered the restaurant, so I assumed she too found them awkward. Worried that inertia was about to set in, I made a random comment, "Do you remember before restaurants were all chains? You know, when some were stand alone businesses."

She looked up from her device. "Yes, barely. But I do remember my father taking me to an old-timey place where they had human waiters and bartenders. I remember they greeted my father by name. I will never forget that. They were mostly gone by the time I was an adult." She seemed lost in thought for a moment, then her attention returned to her device.

We slowly walked toward the side of the room where the wall was covered with a grid of little glass doors. "Here it is," Sarah said, still looking at her device. She entered her order by tapping its screen. As we approached the wall, one of the glass doors flew open. In the cubicle behind the glass door was a plate of spare ribs. She pulled it out, looked at me and said, "The real thing." Then she inhaled deeply over the plate and smiled broadly. "Have you found something yet?"

"Yes," I replied, and after a tap on the screen of my device another door flew open and I collected a French Dip sandwich. *Damn!* I wanted the ravioli, but due to nervousness I wasn't paying attention and I tapped the wrong menu item. It wasn't the first time this happened to me, so I knew it was too much trouble to exchange it for the dish I wanted, plus there was a charge for returned meals. I decided, as I usually did in such cases, to just eat what I got. *How bad could a French Dip sandwich be?*

After we got our drinks Sarah said, "Over there," indicating an empty table with a nod of her head. She took a seat and I sat across from her.

I looked around the near empty room. "Looks like we picked a good time to eat," I commented, as I took the first bite of my sandwich. It was a bit on the dry side.

She rearranged a bite of spare ribs in her mouth, then replied, "Yes, I always try to hit this place about this time of day, otherwise it is crowded and there is no place to sleep. I mean sit," she quickly corrected herself, then wiped her mouth with a napkin.

Was that a Freudian slip? I wondered, but made no mention of her comment, it was our first in person date after all. I looked at my surroundings and saw that toward the back of the room there was a short line of people dressed in rumpled, ill fitting clothes. I'd seen such lines before and always assumed they were people who wanted to buy the discounted meals that had been mistakenly ordered, then returned. *They look like u-bees or menials,* I thought. Menials were people who did menial work, like the greeter in The Barbary Bistro. I turned my attention to the greeter.

"A penny for your thoughts," Sarah said.

"Oh, sorry. I was just looking at the greeter and wondering who thought that his costume looks like Old San Francisco," I explained my distraction.

"Well, for most people, how would they know the difference? Not everyone is a fashion expert," she teased me. "So... how is the sandwich?"

"Good, if you dip it in the sauce," I said, dipping my sandwich into the ramekin. Before taking a bite I looked up from my sandwich and directly into her eyes, "Sarah, would you like to go for drinks after dinner?"

"Sure I would. I was going to bring that up myself... Once I finished my ribs, that is," and she went back to eating.

After bussing our plates, so as not to receive a dirty look from the greeter, we walked back out onto the street. "Johnny Boy, it is Saturday night and our first in person date, how about I splurge for a red-car," Sarah said. "I just got transferred to the Uni-Gon in Cupertino. I got a big raise and I want to spend it like I got it."

A red-car is a very fast auto-car. They are also very expensive. I'd only been in two or three in my life. We waited at the curb for a few moments, then a sleek red-car pulled up with a screech of its tires. The door opened and Sarah slid into the seat. "This one was just cleaned," she said with delight.

"Yeah, smells like it," I agreed, as I slid in next to her. "They keep these beauties spotless. So, where to for drinks?"

"Are you in the mood for something different?" she asked.

"Sure, I am up for anything," I replied.

"Well, are you up for something really different?" she smiled.

"Yes. Why not? What do you have in mind?"

"So... a couple of years ago I was dating this guy and he took me to this really old place, I mean it is an antique. I have not been in it since then. Your comment about 'stand alone businesses' is what made me think of it."

"Is it safe?" I asked, beginning to worry about her plans. I'd had first in person dates with women I dated online and sometimes they turned out to be very different in person.

"Oh, stop worrying. It will be fun," she replied.

Her answer didn't reassure me but, throwing caution to the wind, I replied, "Sure, why not?"

Sarah tapped our destination into her device and I was immediately pinned to the seat-back of the red-car as we turned left onto Market Street. As we headed north I was reminded of how fast red-cars traveled. With all of the auto-cars on the street controlled by the XG Network, the white, blue, and black cars got out of our way and we were able to move through traffic at a tremendous velocity. We made a left turn onto Kearny Street, where the red-car went faster than I found comfortable, giving me an adrenalin rush.

Halfway up Kearny we swerved around one of the lumbering city busses that the u-bees and menials use, then we slowed briefly as a u-bee jaywalked in front of us. Jaywalking is illegal but it isn't dangerous. So long as you walk slowly and deliberately, the auto-cars avoid hitting you. It's only illegal because it's an impediment to the smooth flow of traffic. Auto-cars of all colors and the busses have to stop at the signal lights to allow cross traffic to pass, but we didn't get caught at one. The signal lights, which are also controlled by the XG Network, are for the pedestrians. The auto-cars stop when the Network tells them to.

Moments later our red-car pulled up to the curb in North Beach and stopped with a screech of its tires. I'd been told that they could stop just as fast without the screech, but research found that people loved the sound, so red-cars always stopped that way. In fact there's a saying, "You do not pay for the red-car, you pay for the screech."

When I stepped out onto the sidewalk my heart was racing and Sarah was laughing, "Wow, that was worth every bit I paid," she exclaimed. As I waited for her to get out, I looked across the street and saw Kerouac's, a bar I had been to several times in the past. Next to it was a pedestrian alley and across the alley was a virtual store front with a sign that read, City Lights.

Some shops were so iconic of San Francisco that they were designated Historic Landmark Businesses. When they went out of business, as City Lights had many years ago, the city council made the building owners display a holographic image of the original store windows. There could be no displays for people wearing spectaculars or the holographic ads found in most street level windows in the commercial districts. The store front also had to include the original sign and design elements.

When Sarah was standing next to me on the sidewalk we turned toward the buildings that lined the street and found we were in front of a vertical farm. It was a ten story glass cylinder perched on top of an old, red brick building that was recessed from Columbus at the end of a short, dead end alley. Filling the interior of the cylinder were large spiral rails that were visible from the street. Various crops were planted in containers that were attached to the rails on the top floor. The containers slowly rotated down the rails, and when they emerged several weeks later on the bottom floor, the farm menials harvested the crops and they were distributed to restaurants in this part of town. The containers were then hoisted back to the top where they began the process again.

To the left of the alley was a generic building with the typical virtual shop windows. To the right of the alley was a restaurant called The North End Bar & Grill. Sarah walked to the door of the restaurant and held it open for me. "Here we are, Johnny Boy," she said.

I entered and found that The North End Bar & Grill didn't seem very old or different to me. In fact it seemed much like every other high-end place in The City. Though it was situated in an old building, the room had recently been renovated. And it was more expensive than The Barbary Bistro, the smell of roasting beef made that obvious. *No algorithm designed this... they still need us*, I thought with pride, as I admired the stylish decor.

"Here we go," Sarah said, indicating two empty bar stools. We took our seats and used our devices to order drinks. Since this was an upscale restaurant, there was an expediter behind the bar. I watched the Lazy Susan on the back bar as it positioned the proper glass under a chute. The drink and ice cubes were deposited from the chute into the glass. The expediter removed it and began to garnish the drink as the Lazy Susan repositioned itself. When the second drink was finished the expediter garnished that too, then picked them both up and placed them on the bar before us. "Enjoy," she said in a forced cheery tone of voice.

"So what did you think of the red-car?" Sarah asked me, using her finger to toy with the ice cubes in her drink.

"Great. I am still dizzy with adrenalin."

Sarah laughed, raised her glass and said, "To our first in person date." We clinked our glasses together and each took a sip.

"I thought you said this place would be different. What am I missing?" I asked.

"Well, Johnny Boy, it is all about juxtaposition. The next place we are going is the place I told you about. This place is just to set the stage, plus I knew the address of this place."

What does she have in mind? I thought, sipping my weak, expensive, over garnished drink that tasted like nothing in particular.

After we finished our drinks, we left The North End Bar & Grill and went back out onto the sidewalk near where the red-car dropped us off. Sarah took me by the hand and led me into the dead end alley. At the end of the alley was a doorway for the vertical farm. On the left side of the alley there was a shabby doorway with no sign. Around the door a dozen or so people stood smoking hand rolled cigarettes.

We walked through the crowd of smokers, who reeked of tobacco and marijuana, then passed through the door and into a room that looked like what The Barbary Bistro was pretending to look like. The room was dimly lit, cave-like and filled with all sorts of old photos, mementos, signs, flags, and trinkets which were affixed to the walls and ceiling. It looked dirty. The patrons, of which there were over twenty, also looked dirty and disheveled. I leaned in close to Sarah's ear and whispered, "What is this, a u-bee club house?" As I did I got a whiff of her perfume, something that didn't come across in our online dates or in the confines of the smelly white-car.

"No, this is a bar. I forget the name, Hole in the Wall, or something like that. And they have human bartenders, look," she said, gesturing to a man behind the bar who rushed around taking orders and making drinks.

"Are they using… "

"Cash? Yes they are, Johnny Boy. I told you it was an antique."

"Cash still exists?" I tried to remember the last time I saw cash.

"Oh, yeah," she replied. "There is some political action group that will not let the government discontinue it. Something about 'legal tender' or something. Have you ever seen those lines of messy people in the back of restaurants?"

"Yes, of course I have… " I thought for a moment, then added, "There was one at The Barbary Bistro. I figured it was u-bees trying to get one of the discounted meals."

"Not exactly. Legally, retail businesses have to have the ability to accept cash. Those lines lead to a machine that accepts cash payments. Of course poor people are the only ones who still use it. I mean it is so inconvenient," she said, stopping at an old fashioned ATM. She pulled out her bank card and inserted it into the machine, pushed a few buttons and out came cash. "The corporations are in court to stop the printing of cash and are expected to win, so cash will probably not be around much longer," she said, removing the wad of bills from the ATM. "My god, look at these."

I looked at the bills in her hand, but they just looked like cash to me.

"These bills are ancient. Look at the president, he is a pin head. There are no anti-counterfeiting strips or anything. And look, they are dated, 1969. That is almost one hundred years! Oh well, what do you want? I am buying. Oh, and keep it simple, they do not make elaborate drinks in this place," Sarah said.

"Thanks, I prefer simple anyway. Make mine a gin and tonic," I replied, and took a seat on a bench against the wall, facing the room. Sarah went to the bar to order our drinks. As she did I watched her. She had a very sexy walk, something else that didn't come across in our online dates.

While I watched her, my attention was diverted to a well dressed young woman who seemed out of place. She was seated at the bar near where Sarah was trying to get the bartender's attention. An old man with a white goatee who was wearing a hat walked in and took the empty bar stool next to the young woman. I was surprised when he said something to her, since he was obviously a u-bee and she obviously was not. I was even more surprised when she replied and they began a conversation. It seemed that the old man knew a number of the other customers, because he occasionally interrupted his conversation with the young woman to greet them. Each time he did the young woman looked to the front door, as if she were expecting someone.

My attention was diverted from them when Sarah returned with our drinks. "When was the last time you had a drink made by a human bartender?" she asked, then handed me my drink and sat in a chair across the table from me.

"I think the last time is when I ate at a top-end restaurant with… " I hesitated, realizing that the occasion I was speaking of was on my last in person date with a woman and I wasn't comfortable mentioning that. "… a friend. That was about a year ago."

"Well, it has been longer than that since the last time I paid for anything with cash," she said, waving the bills in the air to illustrate. "So what do you think of this place?"

"Like you said, 'It is an antique,'" I answered, though my attention was again drawn to the young woman at the bar seated next to the old man in a hat. The old man stood abruptly and walked to the back of the barroom where he stopped by an upright piano. Leaning against the piano was another old man, who had long, white hair and was wearing a gray overcoat. They began a conversation.

A moment later a young man entered the barroom. "Alice," he called out, and the young woman at the bar who I'd been watching stood to greet him. After they hugged, he drew back and said something that I couldn't hear. She shook her head, then said something as she gestured, first to her half-full drink sitting on the bar, and then to the empty bar stool recently vacated by the old man in a hat. The young man grabbed her hand, forcefully pulled her to the door, and they were gone.

"Hey, Johnny Boy. Here I am."

"Oh, sorry Sarah, I was distracted by a scene at the bar," I explained my fascination with events unfolding before me.

"I know what you mean, this place is great for people watching. But come on, this is our first in person date, pay attention to me." She held up her drink and we clinked our glasses together, then each of us took a sip.

"Oh! I asked the bartender about these old bills. He said the Feds have stopped printing cash because the corporations are going to win in court. The local reserve bank has been going into their vault and finding cash that has been stored in there for years. They recently worked their way down to bills that were on the bottom of the pile. He said when the owner went to the bank to get cash to refill the ATM, these are what they gave her," she said, holding up her wad of bills for a moment, then putting them into her pocket.

"Bank? You mean a brick-and-mortar bank? I have not seen one in years," I replied.

"Yes, downtown. There are a couple of them, but you would

not notice them, they are behind anonymous facades. You have to know where they are to find them," Sarah explained.

I was wondering how she knew so much about cash and banks when the crowd of smokers returned to the barroom, bringing the smell of tobacco and marijuana with them. This influx caused a hub-hub as the patrons reshuffled themselves to make room for the returning smokers. Sarah was getting jostled as people brushed passed her, so she got up from her chair and moved around the table to sit next to me on the bench.

"This is more comfortable. Besides, I like to people watch too," she said, squeezing my thigh with her free hand.

"Much more comfortable," I responded, sensing I was becoming aroused by her touch.

"Look at all of these useless-bits," she used a derogatory expression for u-bees. "This is hilarious, everything is so inconvenient." She leaned in close, then whispered, "And a few of them smell like the white-car."

Nervously grasping for words, I commented, "These drinks are strong." *It's now or never,* I thought. I lowered my drink to the table, turned my head and kissed her on the lips.

"Oh, John, I have been waiting for that for a long while," she said, when I came up for air.

"Me too," was all I could think to say, then added, "I am dizzy all over again."

Sarah laughed, then her tone changed to one of concern, "Uh-oh, Johnny. An old man is eyeing our table... and here he comes."

"Hey you two, get a room." I turned my head as the old man in a hat that I'd been watching at the bar stepped in front of our table. He had a smile on his face and appeared to be drunk. "Mind if I share your table for a moment?" he asked.

"So... this is our first in person date," I stammered, surprised by his request.

"Oh, I won't be here long, just waiting for an empty bar stool to open up," the old man assured us.

I was thrown off by his forward behavior. Generally, in the bars I was used to, people didn't talk to people they didn't know. They certainly didn't invite themselves to sit with a couple. But I was out of my element and decided it would be best to just go along. "Yes. Sure," I answered.

He pulled out a chair, sat on it, then scooted in. The legs of the chair chirped as they slid over the cement floor. "I haven't seen you two in here before, have I?" He asked, then took a sip of his beer.

"I have been here once before, but that was a while ago," Sarah answered. "I dated a guy who came here. He is the one who introduced me to... What is the name of this place?"

"The Rabbit Hole," the old man answered.

"Oh yes, The Rabbit Hole."

"What's your friend's name? Maybe I know him," he asked, adjusting his hat to a slightly new angle on his head, saying as he did, "I'm always in here, it's one of the only real bars left."

"Jarad. He works in security at the detention center over on 3rd Street," Sarah answered.

I was surprised to hear that she had dated a menial. I made no mention of it, but it did solve the mystery of how she knew things that people in our social strata usually didn't know.

"Jarad. Oh yeah. A tall menial, right? I think I know him. He still comes in here, mostly on Sunday nights, if I remember correctly," the old man said, pulling on his white goatee.

"Yes, that is him. He brought me here a couple of years ago on a Sunday night. I was not sure if this place still existed or if I could find it."

"Well, it probably won't last much longer, the bankers will see to that. Them and the mega corporations. They want everything and in the end, they'll get it. The owner of this place is an old woman named Mona Lisa who inherited it. That's her over there," the old man pointed out a woman sitting near the back of the barroom. "This bar was started by her grandparents. They were an old lefty couple who stipulated in their will that this place would never accept bank cards or any sort of payment other than cash. Its days, like mine, are numbered," he told us.

"Oh... That is too bad," Sarah replied with obvious discomfort.

"It's the way of the world, missy. Now that the mega corporations run things and the government is a joke, they do whatever they want. They'll be taking our money away soon and then we'll all be screwed. Look what happened to Sweden after they took the money away," he ended on a somber note.

His comments were beginning to cause me discomfort as well, so to change the subject before he ventured further into forbidden speech, I introduced Sarah and myself.

"Sarah, John, pleased to meet you. People around here call me Hatter. I used to sell hats on upper Grant Avenue years ago at a place called Poor Taste. I've been living in this neighborhood for decades and I remember when this was a real neighborhood with real bars. Then, back in the teens, new money came to town and gutted this city. What it didn't destroy, the pandemics that came shortly after finished off. I'm amazed any single location business survived. Most of the bars around here now are Disneyland affairs, not worth going into, in my opinion." At this point the old man craned his neck to scan the bar. "Oh, there's a bar stool. A pleasure folks." With that he rose and moved to the bar.

I remained mute until after he was seated. "Did you find that weird?" I asked Sarah.

"A little bit," she replied. "The u-bees do things differently, but we were looking for something different." She took the last sip of her drink, wrinkled her nose at me and said, "I need another. You want one?"

"Sure. Let me get it. What do you want?"

"Same as before, bourbon rocks."

I pulled my device from my pocket and prepared to order our second round.

"Put that away, Jonny Boy, it will not work here. They only accept cash and you have to order directly from the bartender," Sarah explained.

"Really. You mean Hatter was telling the truth? Oh well, I will be right back." I slipped off the bench and headed to the front of the barroom where the ATM was located.

I pulled my bank card from my pocket. I hadn't used it much in years, I paid for everything with my device or facial recognition. The only reason I carried it was for identification. Bank cards had replaced driver's licenses as the primary form of legal identification when people stopped driving. I had heard

that they would soon make devices the primary form of legal
I.D., but for the time being it was still banks cards. I was leery of
using it in the ATM because, with some regularity, a story turned
up online about a hapless person who lost their bank card in an
ATM. If that happened I would be without primary identification, an unsettling prospect. After convincing myself that it
would be safe, I slid my card into the slot. I withdrew four hundred dollars, figuring that should be more than enough to cover
the drinks we'd have in this place. The machine disgorged a stack
of crisp, twenty dollar bills, which I quickly put into my pocket.
As I did someone tapped me on the shoulder.

I turned and saw the old man with white hair that Hatter
had been talking to by the piano. "Excuse me, I know you don't
know me, but I'm a friend of Hatter's," he introduced himself. "I
noticed that you know him too. I have a favor to ask of you; my
sister is sick and I don't own a device. May I borrow yours for a
short voice call? I really need it."

"Well, actually I just met Hatter... " *My device? This guy has
some gall.*

"From each according to their ability, to each according to
their need," he said sweetly, in an obvious attempt to sway me.

Well, as Sarah said, 'The u-bees do things differently.' Why not? I
pulled out my device and activated it. The screen lit up displaying
the time as *8:09* P.M. I tapped the phone app, before handing it to
him, saying as I did, "Okay, but do not take too long."

"Thanks, I won't. What's your name?" he asked, holding out
his hand.

"John, John Simon," I replied, shaking his hand as I did.

"I'll be right back, John," he said with a thin smile, then turned
and headed toward a doorway at the back of the barroom. "I want
to go somewhere where it's quiet," he explained over his shoulder.

He never told me his name, I thought, as I watched my device disappear through the doorway. Feigning indifference, for
my own peace of mind, I shrugged and approached the bar.

A few moments later the bartender came to me. "Gin and
tonic and a bourbon rocks," I ordered our drinks, then asked
"Where does that door lead?"

The bartender looked where I indicated as he poured our drinks, "The toilet," he answered, then placed the drinks on the bar in front of me. "Thirty-five bucks," he said abruptly, in a tone that wasn't a forced cheerful one. In fact I found him to be gruff and rude, it was as if this menial felt he was my equal. However, I couldn't believe how cheap the drinks were. I gave him two twenties and received five singles in change.

Way over-estimated how much money I would need, I thought, as I put the change into my pocket and returned to our table. "Here you go," I said, handing Sarah her drink. After clinking our glasses together and taking a sip, I told her I was concerned because I loaned my device to an old u-bee who disappeared into the restroom.

"Oh, you are such a worry-wart," she said. "This room is built into the side of a hill, there is no back door, where is he going to go?"

Five minutes later I was worried. "My whole life is on that device," I complained to Sarah.

"So go check on him," she replied, with a slight tone of annoyance.

"Yeah, I better," I agreed and got up, leaving my drink on the table. I went through the door which led to an *L* shaped hallway. I followed the hallway back to the restroom and quickly glanced around what appeared to be an empty room.

I panicked. Walking briskly, I re-entered the barroom. I was walking toward the front door when I noticed Hatter seated at the bar talking with another patron. I tapped him on the shoulder, "Excuse me, Hatter."

He turned from his conversation, "Hey, John. What's up?"

"Have you seen that old guy with white hair you were talking to back by the piano?"

"The White Rabbit? Not in several minutes."

"Well, I loaned him my device to call his sister and he took it into the restroom, but I just checked and he was not in there."

"Sister? The White Rabbit doesn't have a sister. I don't think he even had a mother," Hatter laughed, then added, in a theatrical tone of voice, "There's good in The White Rabbit's heart, but there's larceny in his fingers." Then he laughed again.

"What am I going to do? My whole life is on that device," I said.

"Did you check closely? He's probably still in there, check again," Hatter advised me.

I rushed back to the hallway and into the restroom. I quickly scanned the whole room, making sure it was empty. Then I dashed back out of the restroom and into the hallway. I was just in time to see a gray overcoat scurry through drapes that hung at the short leg of the *L* shaped hallway.

I ran through the drapes and immediately stumbled in a dark stairwell. I rose to my feet, felt around in the dark until I located the handrail, then climbed the stairs slowly, so as not to trip again. At the top of the stairs was another set of drapes. I brushed them aside, stepped through and was shocked to encounter a bare breasted woman holding a tray.

"Excuse me," I sputtered, backing toward the drapes, thinking I had entered the wrong room. She gave me no special notice other than to ask if I wanted a drink. I found myself staring at her bare breasts as I declined the offer and she walked away.

I looked around the room and saw a naked woman dancing on a small stage. All of the other waitresses were also topless. *A strip club? That couldn't be, they all went out of business decades ago.* I wandered about until I encountered a large man in a suit with a badge that read, Management. "Have you seen a white haired old man they call The White Rabbit in here?" I asked him.

"Rabbit? Sure, he came through here a minute ago. He went out the front door," he told me, pointing at the door.

I ran out the door and onto a busy street. I looked around to get my bearings and found that I was near the corner of a large intersection. Across the street I saw The White Rabbit looking in a shop window. *Damn, what luck! I can catch him if I hurry.*

I started to jaywalk directly to where he stood, but in my haste I ran into a short, metal pole with a sort of primitive, mechanical clockwork at the top. *What's this?* I looked down the sidewalk and there were a row of these same poles.

Then I noticed something just as strange; at the curb there was a sign posted two meters above ground level that read, SPEED

LIMIT 25. *A speed limit sign? Then these poles must be parking meters. It's been decades since I've seen these things. What's going on?* In addition to those two archaic details, parked along the curb were huge cars of all different types, painted in a variety of colors. Many of them were dirty, as was the street and the sidewalks. A roaring sound filled the air as did a foul, chemical odor that was oddly reminiscent of something from my youth. But the most disturbing detail was that the cars had steering wheels. I looked to the street and my fears were confirmed, the passing cars were being driven by people. *When did this happen? What part of town am I in?*

The traffic was frighteningly chaotic with no sense or reason to it. Cars weaved, horns honked, people yelled from their moving vehicles and tires screeched. The only thing preventing absolute carnage was the ludicrous amount of space the drivers allowed between themselves and the car in front of them. With this mayhem on the street, jaywalking would be foolhardy. I walked to the intersection, hoping the shop window held the attention of The White Rabbit until the pedestrian light changed.

While I waited I looked at the street signs to get my bearings and found that I was at the corner of Broadway and Columbus. *I'm still in North Beach.* That made sense because the red-car dropped us off in North Beach and I hadn't gone far since then. But this looked nothing like the North Beach I knew. *I haven't been here for a while, could things have changed this much? Are they shooting a movie?* I looked around for a camera crew, which was the only thing that would make sense, but there was no camera crew to be seen. I returned my attention to the pedestrian light and the busy street before me. *Broadway? It seems narrower than I remember.*

As I waited I took notice of the building directly across the street which out did the Barbary Bistro in tastelessness. An enormous red sign with the name, The Condor, ran up the front of the building. It included a gigantic depiction of a woman wearing nothing but a bra and panties with blinking red lights where her nipples should be. On the sidewalk below, a man in a suit and hat paced in front of the doorway and proclaimed in a loud, booming voice, "Her tits are as big as your head, and just like a luxury liner, everybody wants to ride her!"

Oh, my god. That man is broadcasting forbidden speech openly on the street! The man's coarse language, the traffic, the stench, and the general street din were making me nauseous. The light finally changed and I ran into the street where, landing flat footed, I stumbled. I recovered my balance and looked over my shoulder as I ran, to see what had caused my misstep. I saw that the corner I had just stepped off had an abrupt curb instead of being sloped, as all sidewalks were at the corner in my experience. Looking ahead to the other side of the street I saw another abrupt curb, which I carefully stepped up onto when I reached it, then turned to my right and looked up Broadway. The White Rabbit was gone.

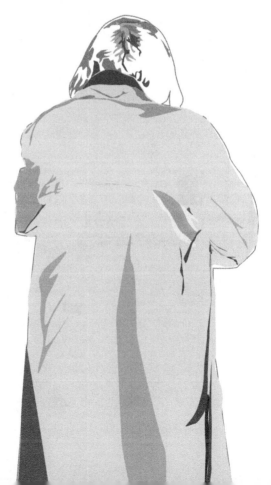

THE CHASE BEGINS
Chapter 2

I PULLED MYSELF TOGETHER AND WALKED QUICKLY UP BROADWAY to get away from the awful man with the booming voice who paced the sidewalk in front of The Condor.

A few more paces and I reached the shop window that The White Rabbit had been looking in when I last saw him. Above the window was a sign that read, The Mystic Eye. Displayed in the window were a row of three apothecary jars filled with some sort of herbs. Behind them unusual geometric images were posted along with several books dealing with the occult.

It's a real shop window. A convenience store? I was reluctant to enter, as I hadn't been in a convenience store since the last time I went shopping with my mother when I was a young man. *The security door won't let me in.* My desire to retrieve my device overcame my reluctance and I tested the door handle. It turned, the door gave way, and I entered the small shop. Bells that were attached to the door jingled, announcing my entry into a room that smelled strongly of something both herbal and floral.

The wooden floor creaked under foot and beneath the herbal-floral aroma that first greeted me, a sour, musty smell permeated the room. *This doesn't seem very exclusive to me,* I thought. On the left side of the shop there was a bookcase filled with books on witchcraft, astrology and other occult related subjects. Just beyond the door was a line of glass display cases which stood a bit over waist high. The cases were positioned three feet from the wall, creating a barrier between customers and the clerk, who was absent.

On top of the case I was standing in front of, there was a wooden box that contained rows of little drawers labeled mugwort, nightshade, and other typical ingredients for witch's brew. On the wooden box was a small, handwritten sign that read, "Eye of Newt and Toe of Frog must be ordered no less than a week before needed."

Gross, I thought. My eyes wandered to the wall behind the row of cases. On it a calendar was posted that read, May 1979. *Huh.* Then I heard a toilet flushing and a moment later a woman with flowing, dark wavy hair, dressed in a colorful peasant dress and wearing a lot of bulky jewelry came out of the back, drying her hands with what appeared to be a paper towel.

Is that a paper towel?

"Hello," she greeted me from behind the cases. "What can I help you with today?" she asked, as she threw the paper towel into a trash can.

"Ah, I am just browsing. Is that an antique?" I asked, nodding at the calendar.

She turned and looked on the wall behind her. "Oh no, that's just a Kit-Kat Klock. It's pretty new, they still make them, but they've been making them for a long time, so the design is old."

On the wall, next to the calendar, was a black and white plastic cartoon cat that had a clock in its belly and eyes that went side-to-side in unison with its swinging tail. "No. Not the clock, the calendar," I corrected her.

"Antique? Hardly. You know, until you opened your mouth I took you for a European tourist."

"Why do you say that?" I asked.

"Your clothes, no one dresses like that around here, but we do get a lot of European travelers in North Beach," she explained.

"Oh, no. I am from here. I live downtown."

"A hotel?" she asked.

"No. A pod," I answered.

"A pod? Oh, I know what you mean, those downtown apartments can be small," she said.

Apartment? What an antiquated expression. But not wanting to get bogged down by small talk, I ignored her comment and quickly launched into my reason for being there, "Has a man they call The White Rabbit been here?"

"Yeah. He stuck his head in the door a minute ago. But he

left, went to Enrico's," she said.

"Where is that?"

"Enrico's? It's a few doors down. It's that big, open front restaurant. I thought you said you live in The City."

"I do. I do. What did he come in for?"

"The usual, to try to sell me something."

"Was it a device?" I pressed her for an important detail.

"You mean paraphernalia? No it was a... Hey, who wants to know? You a cop?" she said, in a tone that was tinged with annoyance.

"No. I am an interior designer. That device is very important to me."

"I'll bet it is. Get out of here. And tell your friends over at Central Station to give their undercover cops better disguises," she said in an angry tone of voice. "I said... Get out!"

ENRICO'S
Chapter 3

S HE WAS QUITE ADAMANT SO I FIGURED I HAD BETTER DO as she wished. I quickly exited the shop, feeling I should put a safe distance between myself, The Mystic Eye and the angry store clerk. I walked briskly up the street, passing a lot filled with cars. The cars were attended by men wearing white smocks with The Flying Dutchman embroidered in red script on their backs. *I haven't seen a parking lot in years, what a waste of space. What's going on around here?*

But before I could solve that mystery, my attention was drawn to a woman coming toward me on the sidewalk. She was wearing an extremely short skirt, high heel shoes, a plunging neckline and heavy makeup. I am not used to this sort of female attire and my gaze lingered longer than it should have. She must have noticed me looking, because she smiled and nodded at me as she passed. I blushed and continued on my way.

When I felt I was a safe distance from The Mystic Eye, I stopped on the sidewalk to plan my next move. As I was doing so I looked up and thought I saw something familiar; it was nearing dusk and a stream of black flying objects sailed high over Broadway. My first impression was they were delivery drones with evening meals for the locals. But I quickly realized they weren't drones, they were crows. *Crows? That couldn't be,* I thought, *the last crow was seen in The City decades ago.*

It was the advent of delivery drones that had chased crows out of San Francisco. I knew this because in college I took an elective on the local flora and fauna. The crows viewed the drones as competitors and would attack them, often with bad results for the crows. More distressing were the drone hob-

byists who attacked the crows for sport. The practice was out-
lawed, but it was a difficult law to enforce and it was enacted too
late to save the crows. The seagulls and black birds had a similar
experience to the crows, so they too left town, though the seagulls can still be seen around the wharf. The hawks, humming
birds, sparrows and pigeons never had much of a problem with
the drones and all still thrive. *Amazing*, I thought, never having
seen a living crow, let alone an entire murder that was obviously
forming. *I wonder how they managed to make a come back?*

"Hey man, you're blocking the sidewalk. Get out of the
fucking way!" A male voice uttered loudly in my direction.

I flushed with anger and embarrassment. I looked to the
source of the gruff utterance and saw a large, filthy man pushing
a cart that was piled high with street debris. His pants hung in
tatters about his waist and, though it was a warm evening by San
Francisco standards, he wore a huge overcoat. I'd never seen anyone quite so dirty and intimidating. I bit my tongue and got out
of his way. *Damn useless-bit,* I thought.

As he passed I looked across the sidewalk and saw a stairway
leading up to double doors. The sign above the entrance read, Finoc-
chio's. Then I looked next door and saw a large, open front restaurant. Above the sidewalk, on a black, canvas awning, Enrico's was
stenciled in white paint. *This must be the place she was talking about.*

I walked through an open space between patio tables filled
with patrons, then entered a room that had tables on the left and
a bar on the right. Most of the bar stools were filled with business
types, but there was an open stool next to an unusual looking
man who appeared to be in his late twenties. He was wearing a
shabby sport coat with an up-turned collar and his temples were
shaved as far back as the front of his ears, totally removing his
sideburns. He was drinking a cup of coffee and smoking a cigarette at the bar. *Even the u-bees don't do that.*

"Are you an undercover cop?" someone asked, as I took a
seat next to the strange man. I looked up and behind the bar was
a hulking man who was looking directly at me.

"No. I am an interior designer," I replied.

"Sorry, but Tatiana from The Mystic Eye called me a minute

ago to warn me that an undercover cop dressed like a European tourist was just in her place and heading my way," he said, eyeing me suspiciously.

"Well that was me, but I am no cop. I am looking for a man known as The White Rabbit. He borrowed something from me and I want it back. Have you seen him?"

"The White Rabbit? Yeah, he just came in to see the manager. He's in the office right now, but you can't go in there," he said. "He'll be out in a couple minutes. And listen," he leaned across the bar toward me, looked me in the eyes and lowered his voice, "I don't put up with trouble in my bar. Is that understood?" he said calmly yet emphatically.

This man was a little over six feet tall, but his real size was in his girth; he had an enormous chest and his biceps were as big around as my thighs. He wore a trimmed beard and his short, blond hair was combed forward into bangs. He wore a light blue, tunic-like shirt that looked homemade. *Probably has trouble finding ready-made clothes to fit him and can't afford bot-tailored clothes.* He gave one the impression he meant business. I assumed he was a menial, but he didn't seem like any expediter I'd ever seen, so I figured he was a security menial, which some bars employ.

"Oh, that is okay, I can wait," I said, reaching for my device to place a drink order, then remembered that The White Rabbit had it.

"Will you be drinking with us tonight?" he asked with a smile.

I realized he was offering to make me a drink. *Another human bartender? Must be a new North Beach thing.* "Yes, I will have a gin and tonic," I replied.

He quickly picked up a glass and scooped ice into it. After making my drink he put it on the bar in front of me. "Three-twenty-five," he said.

Wow, expensive, I thought. *Well, I won't have use for all this cash anyway, might as well pay with that.* I pulled out my wad of bills and began to count out three-hundred and twenty-five dollars. But as I was doing so he picked up a single twenty dollar bill, turned to the cash register, then gave me three fives, a single, and three coins in change. "You mean three... dollars and twenty-five cents?" I was dumbfounded.

"Yeah, Einstein," the bartender replied.

I couldn't believe how cheap the drinks were or that he used coins as part of my change. *This even beats The Rabbit Hole*, I thought, as I picked up the bills and put them into my pocket. *What should I do with these?* I thought, picking up the three coins.

"Hey, I'd leave a tip if I were you," the strange man sitting next to me said.

I looked at him and noticed he had a pencil thin mustache, a tiny patch of a beard under his lower lip and was wearing a gold chain with a strange, gold amulet hanging from it that looked something like a bird's foot print. I also noticed that under his sport coat he was wearing a cadmium yellow T-shirt that was decorated with red and blue rectangles. "How much should I leave?" I asked.

"In this case, I'd just leave the quarters," he answered, then asked, "You visiting from Europe?"

"No. Why do people keep saying that?" I asked, as I put the coins back on the bar.

"Well, no offense, but you got a funny hair cut, your clothes are weird, you speak pretty good English, but like a non-native. And you don't know shit about tipping," was his opinion.

"Well, I live here."

"Where, the Marina?"

"No. Downtown." I was beginning to tire of the subject, so after taking a sip of my gin and tonic I said, "This drink is strong."

"Oh, yeah. Ward pours 'em strong, or as he says, 'I give a generous pour.' You pretty much have to in North Beach, people expect it."

"*Ward*, is that the bartender's name?" I asked.

"Yeah, he's worked here a long time. Ward the Enforcer is what some people call him. You don't want to get on his bad side. But so long as you don't, he's a cool guy."

"Yes, I can see why you would not want to get on his bad side, the man is huge," I replied, looking at the bartender.

"You think he's big, look behind you."

I turned and looked at the other side of the room where I saw an average sized man in a beret with salt & pepper hair and a mustache, sitting at a table with several friends. Then I looked up and hovering behind him was the biggest man I'd ever seen.

He stood only a few inches short of seven feet tall. His face had a strange quality to it, almost like a giant, with a prominent jaw and heavy brow. "Wow," I said.

"Yeah. That's Lucky. He's Enrico's friend. Enrico's the guy in the beret, he's the owner. If you don't want to get on Ward's bad side you don't even want to think about getting on Lucky's bad side. He's bigger than Ward and he's mean too."

"So... what is your name?" I asked.

"Ruben Dann," he said, holding out his hand.

"I am John, John Simon," I said, as I shook his hand. "Ruben, do you know a man called The White Rabbit?" I asked.

"Yeah, sort of. I don't know him well but I know who he is. He's always around The Beach."

"So... he borrowed something of mine and I need it back."

"Can't help you there, like I said I don't really know him. Besides I'm going over to The Mab in a few minutes."

"What is The Mab?" I asked.

"The Mab? It's a Filipino restaurant until eight P.M., then it turns into a punk club at eight-thirty. I think it's past eight-thirty now. Have you ever been to a punk show?"

Punk? Must be something new. "No. Never have been," I answered.

"Well, the Mutants are playing tonight. They're the opening band. They usually headline, but the other band is The Go Go's from L.A. The Go Go's and the Mutants are good friends so the Mutants let The Go Go's have the headline slot."

We were interrupted by a deep, booming voice that came from behind us, "Hey, Ruben, want to help out a starving art student?"

I turned to see a tall, thin man with brown hair and a brown mustache. He was wearing a white T-shirt and denim overalls and was carrying a plastic vase that was filled with cut roses.

"I thought you worked here, Bill," Ruben replied, looking over his shoulder at the man.

"I do sometimes, but it's the slow season so they've cut my shifts. Come on man, buy a rose."

"Bill, what am I going to do with a rose?"

"Give it to one of those beautiful girls I always see you with," Bill suggested.

"I'm going to The Mab. How would I look going into The Mab carrying a rose? Besides, you go to the Art Institute, they ain't starving at the Art Institute. I went to art school at Hayward State on the G.I. Bill. I was always broke, but I didn't starve," Ruben said.

"Alright. How about you sir?" He turned to me.

"How much?" I asked.

"A dollar. You can afford a dollar can't you sir?"

"Yes. Yes I can. Here you go," I said, handing over the single I received in change for my drink.

He pulled out a rose, handed it to me, then asked in a whisper, "Either of you guys want some coke? I got the best prices in town."

Ruben and I both declined, but I pressed him for information, which is why I bought the rose in the first place, "Do you know a man called The White Rabbit?"

"Sure I know him. He owes me for a bindle of coke I sold him last week. He's here now trying to borrow money from the manager, but he's not going to get it. In fact, there he goes now. Hey, Rabbit! Where's that twenty you owe me?" he yelled his last two sentences.

I turned in time to see a gray and white blur streak out of the room, onto the sidewalk and then turn to the left. "Damn! That is him," I said. Leaving my drink and the rose on the bar, I got up and ran out of the door. But by the time I got to the sidewalk The White Rabbit was gone.

THE MAB
Chapter 4

IT WAS DUSK AND WOULD SOON BE DARK. I LOOKED UP THE street to my left, but there was no sign of The White Rabbit. Since the only thing I had to go on was that he turned to the left as he exited Enrico's, I walked briskly up the sidewalk in that direction.

Next to Enrico's was a small restaurant named The Swiss Chalet. I glanced in, but there was no sign of him. I crossed Kearny, which ascended at a steep angle to my left, then walked past a large Italian restaurant named Vanessi's. It looked crowded, but rather than go in and look, I assumed that a man being chased wasn't going to stop off for a plate of pasta.

I soon passed another parking lot, then came to a long row of buildings that had either restaurants or shops of some sort. I was beginning to lose hope when I saw a crowd of people on the sidewalk just ahead. *I hope he's there, I have to get back to The Rabbit Hole, Sarah must be wondering where I went.*

As I approached the crowd I realized they were waiting in line to enter some event at a place called The Stone. Every person in the line was young and wearing black clothes adorned with metal studs and chains. Most were wearing boots and almost all had long, black hair, lots of it. But there was no one who looked remotely like The White Rabbit.

I stopped to consider what I should do next. As I pondered my dilemma my eyes were drawn to a back lit sign that was on a building across the street which read, Mabuhay Gardens. Below the sign, on the sidewalk in front of the building, stood a line of people waiting to enter. The White Rabbit was at the front of the line.

Broadway was choked with cars that inched along in the heavy traffic. Though it was slow moving, I wasn't willing to risk crossing through traffic controlled by human drivers, as all of these cars seemed to be. *Since when are cars driven by humans allowed in The City?* To my knowledge, the closest crosswalk was back at Kearny Street near Enrico's, so I ran back there to wait for the light. As I waited I looked across the street. On one corner was a place called The He and She Love Act. *What could that possibly mean?* My idle curiosity was diverted when Ruben Dann walked up and stood next to me. He was holding my rose.

"Did you find him?" he asked. "Oh, did you want this?" he held up the rose.

"No, you can have it. And, yes, he is in line across the street at the Mabuhay Gardens."

"Well, that's where I'm going, come with me," he said.

As we waited for the light I noticed that one of Ruben's shoes was painted black, the other was painted white. The light changed and we crossed the street together, then walked a block from Kearny Street to the Mabuhay Gardens. The line I had seen from across the street was all but gone.

"Hey, Mark," Ruben greeted the doorman, who had short, dark hair and appeared to be in his early twenties. Mounted on the wall behind him was a black and white sheet of printed paper that read, "The Fab Mab entertainment schedule, May 1979. "

1979 again. Coincidence?

"Nice rose, Ruben." Mark the doorman commented.

"Yeah, it's one of Bill's roses," Ruben said, holding up the rose for a moment. "Mark, this is a friend of mine, John. He's cool."

"Visiting from Europe?" Mark the doorman asked, as he checked me out, up-and-down.

"No. I am from here. I live downtown on Sutter Street," I replied.

"Yeah, sure. Two bucks," he said.

I pulled two singles from my pocket and handed them to Mark the doorman. As I turned to enter he said, "Not so fast. Give me your left hand." I held out my left hand. "Turn it over," he instructed me. I did and he stamped me on the inner wrist with some sort of simple printing device that left a slightly

smudged *21* in black ink. "Just go in, Ruben," Mark the doorman said, as he stamped Ruben's hand.

We entered a dimly lit room that smelled like some sort of
ethnic food I couldn't identify. The air was filled with tobacco
smoke, music was playing on a sound system at a moderate volume. We walked down a wide entryway, which opened into a large
room. To our left was a raised area with booths where people sat
talking and drinking. Beyond the booths, against the far left wall of
the restaurant, a man stood at what looked like a tilted black table
with rows of levers that he was adjusting. In front of the booths was
what I guessed to be a dance floor, where people stood waiting for
the show to begin. In front of the dance floor was a low stage.

I followed Ruben to the back of the room. Against the wall
on the right was a bar where we went to order drinks. Ruben ordered a bottle of beer called Budweiser. As he was paying for it I
looked at a menu posted on the wall behind the bar. Since most
of the males seemed to be drinking beer, and not wanting to
stand out more than I apparently already did, I ordered a beer
called San Miguel. The bartender put a squat, brown bottle on
the bar and said, "Buck-fifty." I handed him a twenty.

"Got anything smaller? I just opened my drawer," he said.

I took back the twenty, pulled the wad of bills from my
pocket and plucked out a five. When he gave me my change I put
the bills back into my pocket and left the two coins as a tip.

"I see you're getting the hang of tipping, John," Ruben said.
"Let's stand over there," he indicated an area near the dance floor.

We walked away from the crowded bar area and stood near
what I guessed was a loudspeaker. However this speaker was an
enormous affair; it was well over a meter high and it rested on a
pedestal, which made it look even bigger. We began a conversation,
in which Ruben explained the local punk rock scene and the
Mabuhay Gardens to me. As we were talking I heard a high-
pitched, feminine voice say, "Hi Ruben."

I turned, and standing behind us was a gorgeous young
woman with straight blond hair, wearing a very short dress and
high heels. I tried my best not to stare.

"Hey, Holly. How are you, beautiful? Here, I got this for

you," Ruben said, handing her my rose.

"Gee, thanks! I'm great," she said, in a flirtatious tone of voice as she accepted the rose. "Where's Kelly?" she asked.

"Him and Libby are down south, visiting his family. They should be back by Tuesday, that's my 30th birthday," Ruben answered.

"Well, happy birthday, if I don't see you again before then. Who's this guy?" she asked Ruben.

I looked up and flushed with embarrassment, realizing she had caught me looking at her legs.

"This is John, and he's not visiting from Europe," Ruben replied, accenting the word *not* and speaking in a comical tone of voice. "John, Holly, I want to get a good spot by the stage, see you guys in a while." Ruben wandered away leaving me with Holly.

"So did you come to see the Mutants or The Go-Go's?" Holly broke the ice.

"Actually neither. I came in looking for a man called The White Rabbit. Do you know him?"

"No. But... Oh hi Ruby," she cheerfully greeted someone behind me.

I turned to see a woman with short hair, half of which was dyed a bright unnatural red, the other half bright green. "Hi Holly," she said. "Here to photograph the bands, as usual," she said holding up what appeared to be an antique film camera with a large lens attached. She spoke with what I guessed to be an up-state New York accent. I took an elective in college on regional accents of the late 20th and early 21st centuries and did quite well in the class. Hearing Ruby's accent, which to my knowledge no longer existed, added to my growing suspicion that something was amiss.

"Who are you shooting for now that *Search & Destroy* is no more?" Holly asked Ruby.

"Other than for myself, *Slash* called me from L.A. Their photographer's car broke down on his drive up. They didn't have time to get another photographer up here so they called me. I'll actually get paid for this gig. Besides, Vale's already working on a new project, so he'll be needing photographs. Where'd you get the rose?"

"Ruben gave it to me. Oh, Ruby, do you know a guy called The White Rabbit?" Holly asked for me.

"The White Rabbit? Yeah, I know him," Ruby said in a

weary tone of voice. "More like The White Weasel if you ask me. Oh, hi Vale," she greeted a man who joined us. For a moment they embraced, kissed, then parted to stand next to one another.

"Hi Holly," Vale said. I noticed there was a nasal quality to his voice. He was Asian, dressed in all black and his hair was cut in a sort of bowl cut. He said a few more things to the women, but I didn't pay attention to what he was saying because I was distracted by the way he spoke. He had a strange regional accent that I was unfamiliar with. In addition to the nasal quality in his voice, he dragged out his words, twisting and emphasizing each one in an unusual way. *I wish my professor could hear this guy.*

Before Holly could introduce me, if she was going to, another man joined the growing crowd. When he greeted members of the group, I noticed that he spoke with the same nasal accent as Vale. Thinking I might be able to identify an accent new to me, I leaned in close to Holly and asked, "Are they from the same place?"

"Because of their accents? No," she laughed. "A friend of mine says that they're the only two people on the planet with that accent. The Asian guy is Vale, he's from here, I think. He was the publisher of *Search & Destroy* magazine, they published their last issue a couple of months ago. Ruby's his girlfriend and she's a photographer who used to shoot a lot of the photos for *Search & Destroy*. The other guy's Biafra. He's the lead singer for this band called the Dead Kennedys. I think he moved here from Colorado or some place like that." At this point she leaned in, put her hand on my arm and asked, "John, will you buy me a drink?"

I was taken by surprise, both by her request and the fact that she was touching me. *What does this mean?* I sensed I was becoming aroused. With an embarrassment of the flesh growing in my pants, I was frantic to find some way of hiding it before she noticed.

Misinterpreting the expression on my face, she quickly added, "Oh, I'll pay for it. It's just this." She turned her arm over to reveal a crudely printed black *X* on her inner wrist. "I'm not twenty-one," she said with sad, pleading eyes.

"Yes, yes I will," was the only reply I was capable of.

She held out a five dollar bill and said, "Vodka cranberry."

Eager to escape, I waved off her money and quickly turned

toward the bar. At the bar, as I ordered her drink, I was thankful to feel flaccidity returning to my pants. I returned and confidently handed her the drink. She thanked me, then told me she heard the Mutants were running late because their drummer was late.

Before she could explain further we were interrupted by an amplified, rumbling sound. I looked to the stage where a spotlit man stood holding a wand of some sort. I quickly realized it was an old fashioned microphone, complete with the electric cord and mic stand, which was on the stage in front of him. He was balding, wore a trimmed mustache, wire rimmed glasses and, it seemed to me, was built something like a hedgehog.

The hedgehog looked out over the restless crowd on the dance floor toward the back of the room, shielding his eyes with his hand. He made a gesture of sliding the microphone across his throat to the man who stood behind the tilted black table that I noticed as we entered. When the music died down he tapped the microphone with his fingers, which produced a thumping sound. Then he addressed the audience, "How are you animals tonight?"

"Fuck you, Dirk!" a guy in the audience yelled out.

"That can be arranged, talk to my floor manager, Sandra, she'll take your name and number," the hedgehog, who was apparently named Dirk, retorted, his voice amplified by the microphone. A few members of the audience snickered. "Now on to more serious business; I've heard some grumbling around here lately, so I'm throwing the floor open to suggestions for what we can do to improve our service."

"Make the beer cheaper!" a man in the audience yelled out.

"Cheaper? We pay almost three cents a bottle for that beer. I think a dollar-fifty is a reasonable markup. Any other suggestions?" Dirk asked, as chuckles rippled through the audience.

This guy is funny, I thought, as Dirk fielded another comment from the audience.

"Parrrr-ty central," a booming female voice proclaimed.

"Ivey!" Holly exclaimed. I turned to see a woman with short, spiky black hair wearing men's black pants and a black sport coat. She was holding a drink and a lit cigarette in one hand and a stack of printed sheets of paper in the other.

"Hey, Ivey, don't forget you're helping me develop film tonight," Ruby said.

"I know, Ruby. You can count on me," Ivey replied. Then she turned to the others in the group, "Anybody want a calendar? Hot off the presses," she said, taking a drag on her cigarette and a sip of her drink as she offered the stack around. While she was doing so, I took note that the calendar was for June 1979. Everybody took one, folded it and put it into their pocket or purse.

"How about you, man from the future," Ivey asked me.

She thinks I'm from the future? "Sure, I will take one. How much?" I asked. *Are these legal?* I wondered.

"They're free," she offered me the stack. "But don't get too excited, you get what you pay for," she said.

"Thanks," I took one from the top of the stack, folded it and put it into the breast pocket of my jacket.

"Ivey, you think he looks like someone from the future? I thought he looked like someone from Europe," Holly said.

"I thought so too," Ruby agreed.

Vale turned long enough to say, "I'm gonna go with the future," then went back to his conversation with Biafra.

Is he holding two conversations at once?

"Did you see what Vale just did? Kudos Vale," Ivey said. She threw her head back and let out a belly laugh. Then her attention switched again, "Hey Magdalen. Nice of you to show up," she said to a brunette with a pale complexion who joined the group. She was quite lovely, in a quirky sort of way.

"I got mixed up. I thought the Mutants were headlining, so Eva and I went to the Savoy first to see UXA. I already had a drink in my hand when I remembered the Mutants were the opening band."

"Man from the future, this is Magdalen. Magdalen, this is man from the future," Ivey introduced me to Magdalen.

"Yes, I am from the future," I said, deciding to go along with the joke for the time being. I held out my hand for her to shake.

"Pleased to meet you, Futuro," she smiled. Then she took my hand and did a half curtsy.

"Futuro," Ivey exclaimed loudly, then threw her head back for another belly laugh, this one heartier than the first. "From now on I, well technically Magdalen, dub thee Futuro. Did everybody hear that?"

Vale turned from his conversation, "Yeah. 'Futuro.' Got it."

"I do not have a say in the matter?" I protested.

"Nope, too late. Ivey hath spoken; Futuro it is," Vale said, then returned to his other conversation.

"Hey, Futuro," I heard Holly say. I turned to see her smiling at me. "Didn't take you long to get your punk nickname."

"He's from the future. In the future everything happens faster. It takes all the running you can do to stay in the same place—in the future," Ivey proclaimed, then took a drag on her cigarette and then a sip of her drink. "Or here. But what's that got to do with the price of tea in China?" She finished her thought, then laughed.

A woman sidled up next to Magdalen. She was about the same size and coloring as Magdalen, a little thinner and she was wearing bold framed glasses. She was as pretty as Magdalen, though a bit more reserved.

"Futuro, this is my sister, Eva. Eva, this is Futuro, he's from the future." Magdalen introduced me.

Eva's face lit up in a quick, saccharine smile, then went dead-pan just as quick. "I need a drink," she said dryly. Then, without another word, she turned and walked to the bar.

"So are you a Mutants fan?" I asked Magdalen, not knowing how to follow what I took as a slight from her sister.

"You might say that. My boyfriend, Fritz, he's the lead singer," she answered.

I must have looked disappointed, because her next comment was, "But Eva's single."

"I think your sister was unimpressed with me," I replied, pointing out what seemed obvious.

"Oh, that's just New York. We moved here from New York City," Magdalen said.

A man dressed in tight black jeans with a black leather jacket joined our group. His bleached blond hair was combed into a very high pompadour. Under his jacket he wore a black and white horizontally striped T-shirt.

"Oh, hi, Denis," Vale greeted him.

...urt, L. 625 Polk St.
TIAN THEATRE, Leroy & Hearst(1 Block from R.
MABUHAY GARDENS, 980 Market/
ROXIE THEATRE, 443 Broadway/6th St./673-7373
STRAND THEATRE, 16th/Valencia/863-1087/431-3611
YORK THEATRE, 1127 Market/7th St./552-5990
UC THEATRE, 2789 24th St./282-0316.
WEST AUDITORIUM, 2036 University Ave/Sh. Luck. Berk.

TUESDA

MABUHAY
8:30 Japanese theatre
10:00 Controllers
Shakin St. (France)

MABUHAY
8:30 Japan
10:00 YORK (C

FM 92 10-midnite
FM 94 midnite - 1am

FM 92 10-mid
FM 94 mid-1am
2pm. Pacific Film Arch
Duchamp videos F
10:30. Donts @ MAB HAY

FM 92 10-midnight
FM 94 mid-1am

AY'S SALOON
34 ELLIS /STOCKTON
P.M. $2 - DILS
HAY   FILLMORE STRUTS
0's   URGE
MERCY
LOES (TUX MOON - Steve Brown)
10-mid
mid-1am   27 / Punks - F

...e of the Earth

eo ch. 25 & 30 **2**

D plus
STARTED
theatre

UHAY.

30 **9**

UHAY
mitted

MABUHAY
U.X.A.
Blowdriers
Pressure

Punk Rock Movie
@ York theatre

3

MOVIE DAY
QUINTET & ZARDOZ
@ the Roxie

TENANT & DON'T LOOK
NOW @ the Strand

Warhol's FRANKENSTEIN
& DRACULA @ U.C. theatre
Berkeley

10

MABUHAY
BAGS
VKTMS.
T.B.A.

17

WARRIORS @ the Strand
REBEL WITHOUT A CAUSE & EAST
OF EDEN @ U.C. Berkeley
MABUHAY- DEAD KENNEDYS,
BAGS & the UNITS
(tentative) 330 GROVE ST. 9pm
AVENGERS & RAY CAMPI &
ROCKABILLY REBELS
FM 95 2am - 4am

24

NEW YOUTH BENEFIT @
JAMESTOWN HALL
(Fair Oaks & 23rd St. (nr. Dolores)
DAS GASSERS [Zurich]
FILLMORE STRUTS
UNITS 8:30 $2.50
MUMMERS & POPPERS (4)
MABUHAY
GO-GO's
V.I.P's
MANDELLOS
International Cafe
D.O.A.
Rockabilly Rebels (-RayCampi)
Cloyne Court (1 bl. from
Berkeley Rather Ripped)
U.X.A.
MX-80
JARS   (R check on this
one

Clockwork Orange
@ the Strand

KSAN FM 95 2am-12m **4**
330 GROVE ST.
MUTANTS
X
ALLEYCATS
9pm $3

West Auditorium
X-Isles
Jars
Mandellos   9pm $3

FM 95 2am-4am **11**

MABUHAY
MUTANTS (tentative)
Crime
Mandellos
INTERNATIONAL CAFE
X & ALLEYCATS
1839 GEARY 9pm $
DILS, AVENGERS, URGE
9pm $3
FM 101 2am-4am

PACIFIC FILM ARCHIVES (Berkeley)
DUCHAMP Videos 2pm FREE!
MABUHAY
TUXEDO MOON
NOH MERCY
HUMANS

18
FM 101 2am-4am
MABUHAY MUTANTS
GO-GO'S
UNITS
BILL GRAHAM Presents
the SCREAMERS ($6.50)
@ CALIFORNIA HALL (!!)
1839 GEARY
D.O.A.
BAGS
DEAD KENNEDYS
REBELS (minus Ray Campi)
9pm $3
EGYPTIAN THEATRE - midnight
LET THE GOOD TIMES ($2.50
w Chuck Be...

---

the Other Si...
(University & S...
the Jars $

the Front @ Yor...

FM 101 2am-4am
MABUHAY
MUTANTS (tentative)

12

sick.

25

26

"Hi Vale."

"I saw you at the Savoy, aren't you guys playing there tonight?" Magdalen asked Denis.

"We are, but I have nothing to do until we go on at eleven, so I thought I'd come by and flyer the crowd. Want one?" He passed a stack of flyers around. I took one and looked at it, "The Liars, Savoy Tivoli Saturday, 26 May, with UXA and The Offs, Show starts at 9 p.m."

"Well, I better pass these around," Denis said, then turned and walked to the bar.

Magdalen turned to me, "That's Denis, he's the singer for the Liars, but I think they're changing their name to Sudden Fun, this may be their last show as the Liars."

"By the way, Ruby... " Vale began a statement, while his other conversation was on hold because Biafra had gone to the bar. He paused until he had Ruby's attention. Once he did he finished his thought, "Bob Bundy is up my ass."

"Who's Bob Bundy?" Magdalen asked.

"He's our landlord," Vale answered Magdalen's question, then continued his statement to Ruby, "He's pissed because last week the kitchen sink was clogged and Ivey used Drano on it. Of course that didn't work. So a couple of days ago Bob comes to fix it and while he was rolling around on the kitchen floor in his overalls, he rolled in some Drano that leaked out of the pipe he removed and it burned a hole right through his overalls and into his leg." Vale laughed through the last half of his sentence. "The worst part is, it wasn't even my fault. It was you, Ivey and Annex washing your hair in the kitchen sink that clogged it."

"No it wasn't, Vale. It was your coffee grounds that did it," Ruby protested, causing her nose to twist itself to the side briefly, in some sort of nervous tick.

"Oh, give me a break, Ruby. What's going to clog a sink, some coffee grounds or a wad of hair?"

"Coffee grounds," Ruby answered.

"Yeah. Coffee grounds. Well, Ruby, in your heart of hearts you know that I'm... "

"Wrong!" Ruby cut off Vale's sentence.

Vale replied with an exasperated, "Whatever," ending the disagreement for the time being.

At this point a man with a sturdy build and a thin face that was topped with short, black hair that looked as if he cut it himself, walked up from the back of the club to join the group. He wore a jean jacket with the arms cut off to reveal rippling biceps and forearms. "Dave's here," he said.

"Hi Ted, I didn't see you come in. What do you mean, 'Dave's here'?" Vale asked.

"I just dropped him and his shit off in the alley," Ted gestured toward the stage with his chin, where behind Dirk, who was still bantering with the audience, a man with short red hair was lugging a drum kit into place.

That must be Dave, I deduced.

Someone in the audience yelled something at Dave, though due to Dirk's amplified voice I couldn't hear what. Dave waved a hand at the fellow with a grin as if to say, "Give me a break."

At this point Biafra returned from the bar.

"Hey Ted, do you know Biafra?" Vale asked.

"Of course," Ted said, holding out his hand to Biafra.

"Where'd you find parking?" Vale asked, as Ted and Biafra shook hands.

"I just left it in the alley," Ted replied.

"In the alley? You can't park in the alley, Ted," Ivey chimed in.

"I did," was Ted's matter-of-fact reply.

Ivey threw her head back for another hearty chuckle.

A new guy joined the group. He was small and thin, wearing a black, cloth jacket, tight black jeans, a faded, purple T-shirt and black and white, high top, cloth sneakers. His ensemble was topped off with bad dental work on a front tooth, a hammer and sickle pierced earring in his right earlobe and a greasy hairdo that spilled onto his forehead. "Where's the Mutants?" he asked.

"Hey Tim. Dave's late, but he's here now. I just brought him over from Oakland. His car wouldn't start," Ted answered.

"Why am I not surprised?" Tim laughed, then turned to talk with Vale.

"Ted, when is SST playing again?" Biafra asked Ted.

"I don't know, I quit the band. Ask Irene. I'm working on a new band. I need a drink," Ted said, then left the group and walked toward the bar.

"Why aren't the Mutants playing?" a tall man with short, wavy, black hair, wearing black clothes added himself to our group.

"Hey, Mark," Tim greeted the man, then answered, "Dave's late. He's here now, but they're getting a late start. You know those guys from *Sluggo* magazine in Austin, don't you?"

"Yeah. Nick's staying at my studio right now. He was helping me unload my kiln, that's why I'm late."

"Well, could you tell him I'd like to interview him on *Maximum* this week. The show airs Tuesday at midnight," Tim said.

"Yeah, I know when your show's on. But didn't you get a better time slot, wasn't that what the demonstration in front of KPFA was about?"

"We did, but not till next month. June 12th is the first night in the new time slot."

"Cool. Well, I'll tell Nick tonight if I see him. He'd probably love a little free publicity for *Sluggo*."

"Do you have my number?" Tim asked.

"I think so, but give it to me again," Mark said, and they both pulled out pens and went about exchanging numbers.

"Mark, what are you working on now?" Vale asked.

"I'm slip casting 45 caliber semi-automatic pistols," Mark answered, then exchanged slips of paper with Tim.

"45 caliber pistols, what are you going to do with those?" Vale asked with a subdued tone of wonderment in his voice.

"I don't know yet. I'm firing them at higher temperatures than the clay body will support, so they're melting. I have to prop them up with kiln furniture so they droop the way I want. Then they have to be removed from the kiln furniture while they're still pretty hot, otherwise they contract as they cool and sometimes they end up stuck to the furniture. If they do that I have no choice but to break them. It's a real bear to get them off before they cool down because they're too hot to touch with your hands, so I have to wear these bulky asbestos mittens."

"Damn. That sounds too much like hard work to me," Vale said.

"You think that's hard, you should have seen the trouble I had making the slip casts," Mark grinned broadly as he spoke. "I used my own pistol—I'm still cleaning it," he chuckled.

"So these pistols you're slip casting, they sound sort of Dali-esk," Vale said.

"Yeah, Dali updated to the 70s," Mark replied.

The 70s? The evidence was mounting. *How long ago was 1979?* I wondered. Like most people, I had trouble doing arithmetic in my head. I instinctively reached for my device to use its calculator app, then remembered The White Rabbit had it. *I must get it back,* I thought, while scanning the room for any sign of him.

"Well, let me know when you decide what you're going to do with them. I have a new project in the works and we may use photographs of your stuff, depending how things go. It's still in the planning stages now," Vale said.

"I guess things didn't work out with you and Pepe," Mark said.

"No, we couldn't see eye-to-eye. He's doing *Nart* magazine and I'd rather not say what I'm doing yet," Vale answered.

At this point there was a commotion in the entryway. I looked up and saw three people with bulky equipment entering the club. A blond man carried what appeared to be an ancient video camera on his shoulder. A lanky man with short, brown hair carried a tripod and some sort of large, black box. A shapely brunette with a intense aura, had the strap of a bag over her shoulder and a clipboard in her hand.

As they approached our group Vale addressed the blond man carrying the video camera, "Joe, why are you loading through the front door? Don't tell me Target Video lost its side door privileges."

"No," Joe answered with an annoyed look and tone. "Some asshole parked his car in the alley."

"Oh, ha ha," Vale laughed. "That's Ted's car, he just drove Dave over from Oakland because his car wouldn't start."

Joe smiled, "That asshole. He owes me a drink. Where is he?"

"Over by the bar getting himself a drink," Vale answered.

"Perfect," Joe said, as he put down the video camera, then walked in the direction of the bar.

At this point Ruben rejoined the group saying, "I got tired

of waiting around by the stage for the band to start. Dave says it's because his car wouldn't start and... "

"We know, Ruben," Ivey interrupted Ruben mid sentence.

"I'm getting a beer," Ruben said. "I'm going to the bar in the front, there's less of a line," and with that he tossed his empty bottle into a nearby trash can where it landed with a *Bang!* Then he walked toward the front door.

I looked at my own beer. It was still over half full. *Ruben drinks fast*, I thought. A few minutes later I felt the urge to take a leak. "I need to use the restroom, where is it?" I asked Ivey, who was the person standing closest to me.

"They're toward the front, on your left. Go to the women's room, that's where the action is," she answered.

I thanked her and walked toward the front of the club. On the way I ran into Ruben who was walking in the opposite direction with a bearded man who wore a black, brimmed hat that had a snake skin wrapped around the crown. The strap of a large bag was slung over one shoulder. "Hey, John. This is Winston. Winston, this is John," Ruben introduced me to his friend.

"Good to meet you," I said, as I shook Winston's hand.

"Where are you going? Did you see The White Rabbit?" Ruben asked.

"No, just going to the restroom," I replied.

"Use the women's room, it's more fun," he said, then asked, "What's that?"

I looked down at my hand and realized I was still holding the flyer Denis gave me. "Oh, it is a flyer for the Liars show at The Savoy Tivoli," I answered. "You want it?" I offered it to Ruben, knowing I had no use for it.

"Sure," he said taking it from me. "I collect flyers," he added.

"Are you leaving already?" Winston said to someone behind me.

I turned and saw Biafra approaching. "Yeah, we're playing out on Geary at the Temple tonight with D.O.A. and the Bags. Want the rest of my beer?" He offered his half full beer to Winston.

"No thanks, I just got one," Winston replied.

"I'll take it," Ruben accepted the offer. He took the bottle, wiped the top with the sleeve of his jacket, then put it in his side pocket. Then he and Winston walked back toward our group.

I walked to the door of the Women's room, then hesitated. The idea of men's and women's rooms was foreign to me, since in my experience, they stopped using such designations years ago. *Ruben said this was a Filipino restaurant. Maybe Filipinos still mark restrooms for men or women? Or maybe I really am back in 1979. Is that possible or am I dreaming? Or going crazy?* A man and woman came out of the women's room together. *I guess it's okay.*

I pushed the door open and entered a noisy room full of people, both men and women, some sitting on a counter top where the sinks were, others just leaning against the counter top or a wall. The walls were covered with graffiti and nearly everyone present was smoking. I walked past a tall woman, who was rolling a twenty dollar bill into a tube, entered the only vacant stall and closed the door behind me.

As I was relieving myself I heard soft grunting sounds coming from the adjacent stall. I looked at the open space at the bottom of the partition that separated my stall from the adjacent one. There I saw the shoes of two people, one male, one female, that were both facing the back wall. It took me a moment before I realized, *Damn! It's two people engaging in coitus.* Embarrassed, I looked away, finished relieving myself, then zipped up and quickly exited the stall.

I walked past the tall woman, who was now using her rolled twenty dollar bill to inhale a line of white powder off of a small mirror that was set on the counter top. I carefully negotiated my way through the noisy crowd and then out of the smoky, little room, back into the main room.

When I rejoined the group they were gathered around Ruben's friend Winston. I leaned in to see what they found so interesting. In his hand Winston held a long sheet of paper with three black and white horizontal images arranged vertically, one beneath the other. The top and bottom images looked identical to me and the middle image was some sort of night event by a lake.

Winston was explaining, "The top one is a barcode, the middle one is a photograph of a Nazi rally at Nuremberg in the late 1930s. This is a lake and those are klieg lights," he said, pointing at lights that were beamed skyward on the edge of a lake. The light beams were reflected in the lake and looked like a continuation of the beams in the sky. "And the bottom one is what the photo of the rally became after I did about ten generations of photocopies."

"What do you mean by 'generations of photocopies'?" I asked, confused by his statement.

"When you take a photocopy of a photocopy, the image deteriorates a little with each generation. It changes."

I didn't get what made this so interesting to the others. "Oh," I said. Then I noticed an imposing blond, with heavy eye makeup and spiked hair approaching from the entryway. "I hate Mark the doorman," she announced as she joined us. Oh, hi Sam. Hi Jill," she said to the two remaining members of the camera crew who were standing a few feet away, keeping an eye on their equipment.

"Why, Annex. What did he do now?" Ruby asked.

"Well, I say to him, 'I'm on the Mutants' guest list—Annex.' He knows me and knows I used to work for *Search & Destroy* and that I'm friends with the Mutants. But he takes forever looking at the guest list muttering, 'Annex, Annex,' and finally he says, (she momentarily altered her voice to mimic a self-important and ignorant male) 'No, it doesn't appear that you are—Annex.' I said, 'Give me that list,' and I snatched it out of his hand. I look, and one of the Mutants, probably Brendan, put me down as 'Annie.' So I point that out and he gives me a whole bunch of shit about, 'But you told me your name is Annex.' So I said, 'Fuck you Mark! You know me,' and he says, 'I thought that I did,' and gives me that smug smile of his. Finally he asks to see my I.D., but I left it at home, so he gives me more shit. Finally the prick says, 'Alright, you caught me in a good mood. Give me your wrist.' Then the mother fucker gave me an under 21 stamp!" Annex turned over her left hand to reveal a crudely printed black *X* on her inner wrist. "When I protested he says, 'No I.D. You left me no choice. It's a hard law, but it is the law.' And he had that smug smile all while he's saying this to me. I hate that prick."

"Oh Annex, you're just giving him ammunition. Don't let him see that he's getting to you and he'll lose interest," Ruby advised her friend.

"Yeah, Annex," Vale joined in, "You don't walk up to the doorman and say, 'Fuck you. Now let me in free.' That's not how it works."

"Fuck him, I need a drink." Annex turned to look at the bar. "Fuck! And now there's a new bartender—that figures. Oh, there's Ted and Joe. I'll be right back." She walked over to the bar.

"So what's that I don't hear," a large man wearing red tortoise shell framed glasses asked, as he joined the group. Over one shoulder was the strap of a black, leather bag. Over his other shoulder was another strap attached to a large camera.

"That's the Mutants you don't hear, Hugh," Tim answered.

"And why don't I hear the Mutants, Tim? I thought I was late," Hugh said, in a tone of mock self-righteousness.

"Hugh, you're always late," Tim laughed. "And you don't hear the Mutants because Dave is also late, proving that old adage, 'The drummer is always late.' Ted just dropped him off and he's setting up now."

"Oh, so I guess that means I'm not late after all, Tim, which disproves your hypothesis," Hugh said, then he looked at Ruben. "Hello, Squire. Isn't your birthday coming up?" he asked.

"Yeah, on Tuesday," Ruben replied. "I'll be 30."

"Well then, three years and four months from Tuesday you can celebrate your 33-1/3 birthday," Hugh said, grinning.

"Hi Hugh," Holly greeted the photographer.

"Hey, Holly. How are you?" Hugh responded.

"I'm fine. You here to photograph the Mutants?" Holly asked.

"And The Go Go's, if they ever actually play. Holly, let me take a couple shots of you."

"Okay," she said, then struck a glamorous pose, with the rose held next to her face.

Hugh snapped a dozen photos, directing Holly to change her pose several times.

"If they come out good can I get copies?" she asked.

"Sure, Holly," Hugh replied. When he finished he lowered his camera back to his side. "Who's this," he asked, looking at me.

"That's Futuro. He's new. He's from the future," Holly replied.

"Pleased to meet you, El Futuro," Hugh said, holding out his hand and grinning in a way that turned his eyes into thin slits.

As I shook his hand, Ivey threw her head back and laughed, "El Futuro! Oh! Oh! Oh, Hugh, you're a genius."

Hugh chuckled, turned for a moment to look at Ivey and

said, "That's evil genius to you, Ivey." Then he turned back to me, "So, El Futuro, where are you from? I mean really."

"The future," I said, thinking the Futuro thing seemed to work to my advantage with this group. Besides, I had more important things to worry about. "I am looking for a man called The White Rabbit. Do you know him?"

"No. Is he from the future too?"

"No. Well, sort of. He lives in North Beach. He borrowed something of mine and I want it back," I did my best to explain.

"Well, I live in Albany, that's north of Berkeley, so I don't know all of the local North Beach characters," Hugh said.

"I know where Albany is, I was born and raised there. But I live here in San Francisco... in the future," I said. *Do I really believe that? How could I? What's happening to me?*

"Okay. So what do you do in the future, El Futuro?" Hugh asked, moving in closer to speak with me.

"I am an interior designer," I replied.

"Just an interior designer? Not a space explorer?" He moved in closer yet.

I ignored his condescension and answered, "Yes, just an interior designer," as I backed away from him.

"Uh, okay. You're really from Sweden, aren't you?" Hugh asked, moving in closer again.

"No, as I said, I was born and raised here in the Bay Area," I replied, backing up to give myself more space between us.

"He he he," Hugh laughed with a squeaking little giggle, which was out of place on a man of his size. "So why do you talk like a cone head?" He asked, a huge grin distorting his face.

"What do you mean by cone head?" I asked, sensing that *cone head* was a pejorative term.

"Well, you speak very carefully and you don't use contractions. You know, like the cone head aliens on Saturday Night Live who are trying to pass for Earthlings."

His second sentence made no sense at all, so I ignored it and addressed his first sentence, "My mother taught me to speak clearly and, most importantly, not to use contractions. She scolded me whenever I did, saying that I would never get a good

job. In my workplace using a contraction can get you put on no-tice or even get you suspended without pay. Eventually it will get you terminated."

"Why is that?" Hugh pressed me, leaning in so close that his face nearly filled my field of vision.

What is this guy, a lawyer? "Because it is rude and disrespect-ful to non-native English speakers. Many of my co-workers are non-native English speakers," I explained, backing up.

"Okay, but if no one in the future uses contractions... "

"I did not say no one uses them," I was becoming annoyed by his cross examination so I cut him off. "The u-bees use them all the time, so do the menials and together they make up over half of the population," I explained, backing up against the loud speaker box.

"*U-bees,* what's that?" he asked.

"They are the people who the corporations pay not to work." Anticipating his next question I added, "And the menials are peo-ple who work at menial jobs, like security guards, greeters in restaurants, that sort of thing." *He must know this stuff, why is he being difficult?* "Besides, I use contractions in my head when I am thinking. But I have been trained since I was a child not to use them in speech."

"Okay. That's pretty good," Hugh backed off. "You're not going to break character, are you?"

"There is nothing to break. This is who I am."

"Can I take a photo of you?" Hugh asked, pulling his camera up from where it hung at his side.

"Sure," I said, slightly flattered by his request, and definitely relieved that the cross examination seemed to be over.

Hugh backed away and snapped two quick shots of me. "Thanks," he said, again with a big grin that turned his eyes into thin slits. "Now, when I develop these tomorrow, if you show up in the negatives, I'll know you're not from the future."

At that point my head was swimming, so I didn't bother to respond to his statement.

"Well, I-am-go-ing-to-get-a-drink," he said, mimicking the way I speak. "See you later, El Futuro. Or will I?" Hugh turned toward the bar and another big smile spread over his face. As he walked he called out, "Annex, Mark tells me you're not 21 yet."

"No, Hugh, don't," Ruby said, in a concerned tone of voice, as she rushed over to the bar to mediate what she apparently perceived as a potential problem.

At this point a short, stocky man, wearing a sport coat, white dress shirt and a paisley ascot entered briskly from the direction of the front door. His dark hair was parted and it fell across his forehead. He bore a resemblance to Peter Lori from old movies, including the bug eyes. He took a drag off of his cigarette, then held one finger in the air and, in an affected accent, he loudly proclaimed, "Sven never pays! Grandmama once told me, 'Sven, you should never have to pay for anything,' and I always obey Grandmama."

"Oh boy, Sven's already lit," Holly laughed. "I love Sven," she added, then laughed again.

Mark the doorman was at Sven's side in an instant. "Alright Sven, pay the two bucks like everybody else, or get out, varlet," he said sternly.

"I'm hardly everybody else," Sven sniffed with displeasure. Then, thrusting the hand that was holding his cigarette into the air, he reiterated, "Sven never pays!"

Mark the doorman grabbed the arm Sven held in the air and whipped it behind his back. A shower of red sparks cascaded to the floor from the lit end of the cigarette. Mark the doorman quickly escorted Sven to the front door and back out onto the street.

All the way out Sven protested loudly, "Ow! Ow! Police brutality! Police brutality! Someone get a picture of this!"

I was distracted from this little drama by the sound of the microphone being put back into its cradle on the mic-stand. "Okay folks," Dirk said, "The Mutants were scheduled to start at nine. It's now almost nine-thirty. I assume this is fashionably late enough, even for them. Heaven forbid I get what I pay them for. The only thing that keeps me from getting upset is when I remember that I clipped each one of you morons two bucks a head to get in here."

"Fuck you, Dirk!" a man in the audience yelled.

"Talk to Sandra. Boy, my dance card is filling up fast tonight folks. And now, without further adieu, and I apologize in ad-

vance for what you're about to see and hear up here tonight—
Here... Are... THE MUTANTS!"

As Dirk exited to the right the spotlights rose, seven band
members bounded onto the stage and immediately launched
into their set, "Dut Dut Dut Dut Dut Dut Dut Dut Dut... Syd
is a nightcrawler... "

They were a motley assortment of shapes, sizes, genders and
were dressed in a wide variety of styles. The lead singer was a
short, barrel chested man with shaggy blond hair who wore a
white T-shirt and black slacks. One of the two female singers was
a tall, attractive blond dressed in a second hand evening dress. The
other was a small, cherubic brunette who wore a bright green
plastic rain coat over a black dress with a huge, white, pleated collar, that looked like it belonged on an antique doll. On her lower
extremities she wore black and white, horizontally striped leg-
gings and strange, pointy toed red shoes. Both women had their
hair ratted up into fright wigs and both wore heavy makeup. They
bounced up-and-down and bounded around the stage. Behind
the singers was a line of three men playing guitars. To the left of
the guitar players, against the far wall, was Dave the drummer.

As soon as the band played the first note the floor in front
of the stage became a field of bouncing people. Up-and-down
they jumped, not necessarily in rhythm to the music, but it
seemed to me they were dancing. As I watched it became obvious to me what was going on; since they were viewing the show
from a flat floor and the stage was only knee high, people in the
back could not see the band. They jumped up to catch a glimpse
and then just kept doing it. Most of them were airborne longer
than they were in contact with the floor.

Ruby was perched with her camera in the raised area behind the dance floor. The video crew were near her. Hugh was
toward the front of the dance floor, near the stage, snapping photos at a furious rate. Near Hugh was Ruben, bouncing up and
down, which sort of shot down my theory since he had an unobstructed view of the stage. I noticed that sometimes a person
would bounce sideways and bump into someone else. Occasionally someone would get knocked down. When they did someone
nearby would hold out a hand to help them back to their feet,

and then both would return to jumping up-and-down.

But what really shocked me was the noise level. As soon as the band started, the enormous speaker I was standing near began emitting sound at ear shattering volume. There was another speaker of the same size on the far side of the stage, and smaller speakers mounted on the walls. From all of them combined the music was intolerably loud. I could feel the bass beat in my chest.

This was beyond my experience. In the concerts I'd been to there were usually no speakers, the band members had audio pickups on their instruments and on the microphone. Audience members wore their spectaculars. If you wanted to have a conversation with someone you simply turned down the volume on your specs or took them off completely. If you took them off you could still hear the music, but it was not amplified. What was going on here was totally visceral, animalistic and exciting.

As I was contending with all of this stimuli, The White Rabbit streaked past me, heading toward the back of the room. Just past the bar he stopped at the side door and turned to face me. He lowered his head and was wracked by a spasm of what appeared to be laughter. Then he raised his head and looked at me with a thin smile. He was so close I could see the little white hairs on his face. But before I could make a move, he twirled in place and bolted out the door.

That was when I sprung into action.

Vesuvio
Chapter 5

HEY! THAT'S FOR BAND MEMBERS ONLY," SOMEONE yelled, as I dashed out the door, into an alley where I immediately flopped over the hood of a car. I righted myself and looked up the alley to my right. The White Rabbit was nowhere to be seen. Then I heard a heavy metal door close. I looked across the alley to the source of the sound and saw a metal door that was recessed into an arched, concrete entryway. I ran around the hood of the car, opened the door, then entered a brightly lit game arcade in time to see The White Rabbit run out the front door onto Broadway.

As I ran through the arcade I noticed it was filled with a mixture of huge, old video games like ones I once saw in a museum down in Silicon Valley and ancient, mechanical pinball machines that I'd only seen in news videos or old movies. Dirk was leaning against one of the pinball machines, talking with a couple of young men. I briefly considered stopping to complement him on his earlier performance as M.C., but I had no time to waste.

I ran out the front door and looked to my left. The White Rabbit was about to reach Columbus Avenue. I ran after him, but by the time I got to Columbus he had crossed and the light changed, so I was forced to wait. While I waited I visually tracked his progress. He walked downhill, crossed a narrow alley, then entered an old, two story bar with a backlit sign that read, Vesuvio. I realized it was the bar I knew as Kerouac's, but in a more run-down state. I had seen it in the state I was familiar with only an hour or so earlier when Sarah and I got out of the red-car. *They couldn't have changed its facade that fast, is it possible that it is 1979?*

When the light changed I crossed the street and walked downhill toward the alley. Just before the alley I came to City Lights Books. But this wasn't the virtual store front I had seen earlier, this was the real thing. The lights were on, there were book shelves filled with books and the store was filled with shoppers.

A tall Asian man stood behind the counter, taking cash payment from customers. One of the customers standing at the check out counter was holding a large, and from the way he hefted it onto one arm, heavy box. Then he used his free hand to open the door. He began to exit, but as he opened the door he stopped for a moment, then turned. "Paul, thanks again for taking this delivery. Columbus Books owes you one," he said to the clerk.

"Don't worry about it, Peter, that's what neighbors are for," the clerk said to the customer.

With that the customer continued on his way.

This is definitely a functioning book store. And it's definitely not a convenience store. The evidence is mounting for this being 1979. But how could that be?

I cut short my perusal of the famous, old book store and crossed the alley to Vesuvio. Just like the exterior, the interior was more dilapidated than Kerouac's and so were the clientele. They were a rough bunch of characters in all shapes and sizes with rumpled clothes of varying styles. I knew that the front door was the only door to this building, so I took an empty bar stool near the front to wait for The White Rabbit. I had him trapped.

As I waited I glanced around the room. Kerouac's had been designed to appeal to the tastes of 21st century clientele; the walls were painted a restful, neutral color and were hung with sparse decorations that pertained to the writer Jack Kerouac.

Vesuvio, on the other hand, wasn't sparsely decorated at all. In fact, even more so than The Rabbit Hole, nearly every square centimeter of wall space had been filled with some random image or artifact. And, unlike The Rabbit Hole, this bar had better lighting so it's decor couldn't be ignored. The sections of the walls that weren't covered with artifacts had hand applied treatments done in a technique that I was unfamiliar with. There were fake Tiffany lamps hung throughout the room and above where I was sitting hung an ancient and still functioning gas lamp. In short, it went against everything I was taught in design school.

This certainly was not done by an algorithm, I thought, as I tried to make sense of the decor. *But what human designer would do such a thing?* Then it dawned on me that this establishment wasn't designed at all. *This was done organically!* Piece by piece it had grown together as paintings, posters, artifacts and other items were obtained. *What corporation would take such a risk?* A chill went down my spine, *Unless I'm the victim of some ridiculously elaborate ruse, it must be 1979.*

Remembering my predicament, I pulled myself away from studying the decor. Instead I considered the basic layout of the room. This was pretty much as I knew it; there was a very high ceiling with a mezzanine floor that wrapped around from the front of the room, ran along the right side and finally curved around at the back of the room where a stairway descended from the mezzanine to the ground floor.

When the bartender, a tall man with salt and pepper hair, came to where I sat, I ordered a gin and tonic. A moment later he placed my drink in front of me and said, "That'll be $2.50." I handed him a ten dollar bill. When he returned with my change, I noticed his eyes were a startling shade of blue. I put the bills in my pocket and left the coins as a tip. Then I looked around the barroom and noticed that most of the customers were male. *If this is 1979, San Francisco was known as a gay mecca in those days. Could this be a gay bar?* I wondered.

"Hi, my name is Joe. I haven't seen you in here before, have I?" The man sitting on my right interrupted my thoughts.

"No." I answered, then took a sip of my drink. After swallowing I asked, "Why are there so few women in this bar?"

Joe looked around the barroom. "Yeah, I guess there aren't many women." Then he looked at the clock above the end of the bar. "Well, it's not even ten-o-clock, the girls are still home troweling on the makeup. They'll be here the usual time, around ten-thirty. Oops! Spoke too soon, here comes Janet Planet."

I looked to the door and saw an attractive young woman enter the bar. As she did, several of the male customers greeted her enthusiastically. When she passed our position at the bar Joe asked her, "Off work already, Janet?"

"Oh nooo, just taking a break while the band's playing," she replied. Then she yelled to the bartender, "Hey Danny, give me a shot, will you?" She walked toward the other end of the bar, sat on a barstool, then lit a cigarette.

"That chick's got it top to bottom, coming and going," was Joe's opinion. "She cocktails over at the Mabuhay, but I heard she's looking for work here. Most of the male customers are in favor of that. You know, I been drinking at The Zoo for almost two decades. I used to pull a lot of prime tail out of this place."

Zoo? Tail? What is this old u-bee talking about?

"Some of them were as good looking as Janet Planet. Of course, I'm not as young as I used to be. At my age I only got three choices," Joe said, then stopped talking and looked at me.

I sensed he was waiting for a response. Confused by his discourse, but not wanting to be rude, I hesitantly asked, "What are those?"

"Well, there's old girls. There's fat girls. And there's crazy girls. The crazy girls are the only ones worth fucking, but you got to wake up with them in the morning and I ain't got the energy anymore," Joe laughed at his own joke, then slapped me on the shoulder.

I was too shocked to do or say anything. Before I was able to recover he continued, "What did you say your name was?"

"Oh sorry, my name is John, John Simon," I told him.

"Well, John, I was just kidding. Actually I prefer old girls. You know why?"

"No," I said softly and drawing the word out slowly, feeling as though I were walking into a verbal mine field.

"Because they don't tell, they don't swell and they're grateful as hell," he laughed, slapping his knee sharply as he did.

I blushed and felt the urge to move away. But he drained his drink, got up when he was finished laughing, then slapped me on the back and bid me good night.

Thank god, I thought, taking a gulp of my drink.

The vacant bar stool was soon filled by an even older man. As he seated himself, he looked at me and nodded. "Here you go

Earl, these are on me," the bartender said, as he placed a snifter of brandy and a steaming cup of coffee on the bar.

After taking a sip of each, he turned to me and introduced himself, "My name is Earl. What brings you into The Zoo?"

"I thought it was named 'Vesuvio,'" I responded.

"Oh, it is. But all the regulars call it The Zoo," he explained.

"Oh, because 'suvio, sounds sort of like zoo," I said, to show him that I got it. Then I told him why I was there, "I am looking for a man they call The White Rabbit. Do you know him?"

"Yes, I know him. I tend to keep him at arms distance, if you know what I mean."

"So... I loaned him something and I want it back. Do you know where I can find him?"

"Hmm. That's too bad. I can't help you with that. Do you live here in The Beach?"

"No. I live downtown." I answered, noticing that my drink was already half empty.

"A hotel?" he asked.

"No. I live in a pod... I mean, an apartment on Sutter Street."

"Oh, in the Tender Nob." Earl used the name that my neighborhood was called long before the real estate agents renamed it Lower Nob Hill and then eventually LoNo, which is what I call it.

"Yes, the Tender Nob. And I guess I should also mention that I am beginning to suspect that I am from the future."

"The future? Future what?" His confusion was understandable.

"I live in the future, at least I am fairly certain that I do. If so, quite a few years in the future."

"You don't say. How many years?"

"I do not know. I am not good at doing math in my head. Until this evening I lived in the year 2063."

"Really? That's... let's see... eighty-four years. That is quite a while," Earl said, in a dubious tone of voice.

"How did you figure that out in your head?" I asked, impressed with his ability.

"Easy; it's 1979, that's one year from 1980. From 1980 to 2060 is eighty years. Add the one from the front and three from the back and it's eighty-four years."

"Wow! That is a neat trick."

"It's just arithmetic. Well, what do you see as the biggest differences from 2063?" Earl asked me.

"The streets are really dirty, in disrepair, and they stink. But I guess the biggest difference is the cars. They are a lot bigger and they are driven by people."

"What drives them in 2063?" Earl asked.

"They drive themselves."

"Cars that drive themselves? That is futuristic," he seemed impressed. "Do they fly too?"

"No, that is a 20th century concept. But there are delivery drones, surveillance drones and transport drones. The transport drones are probably what you are thinking of, but they are not called cars, they are called 'lofts,' which is short for 'aloft transport.' They are more like what you would call a helicopter than a car," I did my best to explain something I wasn't all that familiar with.

"Lofts, huh" Earl considered the idea for a moment, then asked, "Do you use them?"

"No, not me. They are very expensive and frankly, I am afraid of flying in them," I told him of my fear of the lofts.

"Huh, I thought a man from the future would feel right at home buzzing around over city streets," was Earl's opinion.

At this point I was nearing the limit of my knowledge of lofts, so I changed the subject, "Another big difference is the way women dress; high heels, short dresses and low cut blouses," I said.

"They don't wear those things in the future? I'm over sixty and I don't know if I'd like that, even at my age. Is it a fashion trend?"

"Sort of, but it is a trend that began back in the 2030s. That is when the xyists formed," I said, relaxing as the conversation moved into more familiar territory.

"What's *zyists*?"

"A male advocacy group, sort of like the feminists. It is spelled with an *X* and a *Y*, as in the XY chromosome. The *X* is pronounced like a *Z*, as in *xylophone*," I repeated, almost verbatim, from a college course I took.

"I see. I've heard of things like that. They usually don't come to much," Earl said.

"No, they never did until the xyists."

"What makes them different?" Earl asked.

"Well, for one thing the xyists are progressive. Most other such organizations tended to be reactionary and were easily shot down by the feminists. Another factor was timing. They initially formed when the feminists were beginning to lose support. That happened when women began making as much money, on average, as men. I guess a lot of women did not see a need for feminism anymore. Then the xyists came along and among their first issues was to say that high heels, sheer tights, low cut blouses, push-up bras, anything that is used to broadcast sexuality, is a form of sexual harassment, not just of men, but also of children, other women, the physically impaired, et cetera."

"How did that go over?" Earl asked, sounding skeptical.

"So... the xyists used something feminists had been saying for years; provocative clothing does not make men look, men will look at women no matter how they dress. That being the case, they argued, women were wearing provocative clothing because they were in competition with other women to be noticed. By that time, from what I remember, some women were wearing nothing but panty hose, stiletto heels and sheer, lacy bras in public. In the xyists opinion the bar needed to be reset. It turned out a lot of, not only men, but women agreed. When the feminists saw an upstart men's group drawing support from both men and women they saw a way to reinvigorate their own support. The xyists realized they needed the feminist's experience and connections. They have worked together ever since, 'rewriting the sex contract,' as they say," I explained.

"So they passed laws against provocative clothing?"

"No. No laws. The xyists felt that laws take too long to pass, then take too long to remove when they become outdated. Besides, you cannot outlaw passive-aggressive behavior and even if you could it would be very difficult to enforce such laws. They simply worked to change attitudes and enact social sanctions, which they felt were more respected than laws anyway. In fact they have a saying, 'There are millions of scofflaws, but few dare to scoff social sanctions,'" I said, surprised that so much of the course material was still lodged in my mind.

"I can see that, would you rather be prosecuted or persecuted?"

I didn't quite get his point, but for the sake of the conversation, I pretended I did. "Exactly," I replied.

"How do you know so much about this?" Earl asked.

"Sexual Relations 101a and 101b were required classes for all first year college students," I told him.

"Huh," Earl said, looking somewhat confused. "Well, what do you do in the future?"

"I am an interior designer," I answered with pride.

"An interior designer? I thought it would be something more futuristic than that."

"No. Just an interior designer, they still need us," I said.

"Well... What did you say your name is?"

"Oh, sorry, it is John, John Simon."

"Well, John, it's not that I don't believe you, and pardon me for asking, but your claim of being from the future is a little hard to swallow. Could you show me something from the future?"

"No, I can not think of... Oh!" I said, remembering my spectaculars. I pulled them from my jacket pocket and put them on.

"They just look like fancy safety glasses. What's that bulge on the right temple?"

"That is the Goldtooth transceiver. And these," I said, taking off my specs and pointing to the two bulbs on the ends of the temples, "are the audio transmitters. They transmit audio signals that are picked up by the bones in my head, then are transmitted to my inner ears."

He gave me a perplexed look, then said, "Let me try them on to see for myself."

"Oh, they are useless without my device and The White Rabbit has it, which is why I need it back. Well, that and a million other reasons."

Earl didn't look impressed with my answer.

"Well, I have my bank card. It has an expiration date of 2066." I reached into my pocket. *Damn!* I realized that I forgot to retrieve it from the ATM at The Rabbit Hole. "I guess I left it in the ATM," I explained, "I am not used to using them."

He gave me a look of suspicion and our conversation withered. As a chilly silence settled over us I felt the urge to take a leak again. "Where is the restroom?" I asked.

"Back there, then downstairs," Earl told me, with a toss of his head to indicate it was toward the back of the room.

I asked him to keep an eye out for The White Rabbit, got up and walked to the back of the room where I encountered a stairwell. I descended the stairs, which were covered in some sort of shabby rubber matting, into the basement. There I found two urinals against the far wall. *Old fashioned 'male only' urinals,* I thought, as I stepped up to the one on the left, because there was a man standing in front of the one on the right. His black hair was slicked back and he was wearing overalls and a plaid shirt. He wasn't using the urinal, he was decorating the wall next to it with hand applied designs. I realized he must be the man who did the wall treatments upstairs that had caught my attention. I was fascinated, but I couldn't see his technique because he was standing with his back to me, blocking my view of his hands and the section of wall he was working on. He seemed to be lost in deep concentration.

Not wanting to break his concentration, I gave up and allowed my attention to wander to a pipe that was attached vertically to the wall in front of me. On the pipe someone had written a vertical line of poetry: "Pole pipe / Water waste / Pipe to discharge waste / Pipe pole."

Wordy poet, I could describe that pipe in less words, I thought, as I zipped up my fly. I left the restroom and returned to my bar stool next to Earl, who sat silently enjoying his drink, apparently lost in thought. "Earl, did you see The White Rabbit?"

Earl looked up, "No sign of him," he said, then went back to his thoughts.

I looked to my left to the short portion of the *L* shaped bar. Several characters were sitting there including two black men; one of them was small, the other was very large. The large man wore a flat crowned, wide brimmed hat with a hat band that had oval, silver medallions attached to it. "Well Bob, I've got to go. I'll try to catch your reading at The Trieste next Wednesday," the large man said as he stood.

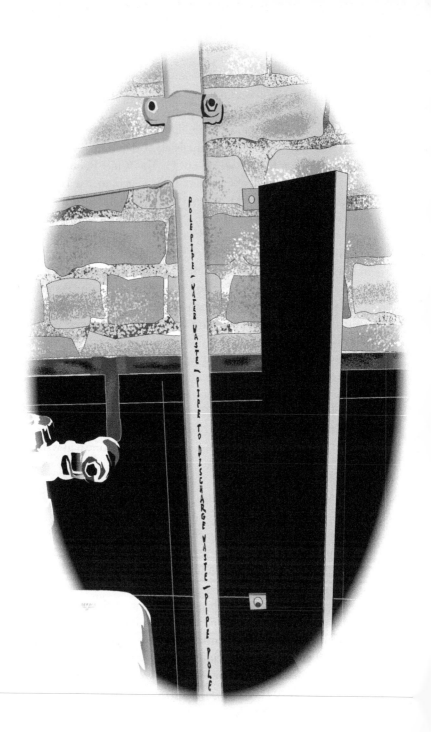

"Thanks, Jim," the small man replied.

Jim was extremely tall, taller than Lucky at Enrico's. Where he was standing the floor of the mezzanine was directly above him and the crown of his hat was only a few inches from touching the bottom of it. He stooped slightly as he turned and slid behind Bob.

The man sitting to my left looked at me and said, "He's over seven feet tall." Then he looked at Jim and asked, "Hey Jim, how's the weather up there?"

Jim smiled faintly, nodded, then said, "Bubba, how many times do you think I've heard that in the last week? The last year? My life?"

"Sorry Jim, I couldn't help myself," Bubba replied.

"Well, Bubba, if you can't help yourself, no one can," Jim smiled, then turned to leave.

As Jim left, another man took his seat. He was also tall, though nowhere near seven feet. He was a white man with dark hair, a beard and a rough look. He was wearing a denim jacket and before taking a seat he turned his back to me for a moment, revealing a design on the back of his jacket. The design included the head of a ram, plus a few other embellishments and the word *Yesod* along the top. Never having encountered the word *Yesod*, I assumed it was his name. Yesod turned to Bob and said something in a conspiratorial manner. Bob reached for his hip pocket and the two made some sort of exchange out of sight, below the bar.

"Ah, taking one of my customers I see, Yesod," a man with a strong New York accent and wildly disheveled brown hair said as he entered the bar.

"The early bird catches the worm, Gregory," Yesod said, without bothering to turn and look at the speaker.

"Hey Danny, who was that chick I saw you with at Vanessi's last week?" Bubba asked the bartender.

Danny replied with just a smile and a wink.

"Well Danny, speaking of Vanessi's, I got to eat. See you later," Bubba said as he slid off his bar stool and ducked under a brass rail that was affixed to the end of the bar. The rail curved up from the bar top, then curved down and was attached to the floor. It was positioned near a gap in the bar that allowed bar staff to enter and leave their workspace. I sensed that the brass rail served to discourage patrons from blocking this gap.

As Bubba left I realized that by sitting with my back to the room I gave The White Rabbit an opportunity to sneak past me. I moved to Bubba's bar stool, turned parallel to the bar and leaned back against the brass rail, giving me an unobstructed view of the rear portion of the barroom.

At that moment a man entered the barroom. "Hey scumbag, you're 86'd," Danny said loudly. The man strode past me holding a raised middle finger while proceeding toward the back of the barroom. "You muther fucker," Danny said, as he came out from behind the bar, bumping into my right arm as he passed me.

The man ran to the stairs in the back of the barroom and ascended to the mezzanine level with an angry bartender following several paces behind. I, along with everyone else, watched as Danny made it to the mezzanine, then came around to stand at the railing above and behind me. I craned my neck to look up at him. With wild eyes and a scowl he scanned the mezzanine for sign of his quarry.

I heard sudden movement upstairs and someone sitting in the mezzanine yelled, "Hey Danny, he doubled back!" Apparently the man being chased had hidden, then doubled back after Danny passed him and was now running downstairs. As the man being pursued ran toward me on the barroom floor, he looked over his shoulder to gauge how much of a lead he had on Danny. Then I felt a loud, *Thud!* and heard, "Got'cha!" behind me. I swiveled on my bar stool and saw that Danny had dropped from the mezzanine into the path of the fleeing man, who ran into his open arms. Danny clenched his teeth in an angry grin as he took the man in a head-lock and dragged him, kicking and yelling to the barroom doors, which he butted open with the top of the man's head.

Adrenalin coursed through my body. With all of the excitement I wasn't paying attention to anything else. A streak of white caught my attention and I saw The White Rabbit's back as he ran out the barroom doors that were still swinging from the impact with the man's head. I jumped up and ran after him. When I was outside I saw him running up the street past City Lights. As I crossed the alley I looked to my left and caught a glimpse of a man laying in the alley groaning and Danny calmly walking back to the front door of Vesuvio, now with a satisfied grin on his face.

I ran to the corner and saw that The White Rabbit had crossed Broadway and was continuing up Columbus Avenue. When the light changed in my favor, I ran across Broadway. On the other side I had to step up onto a small traffic island that was separated from the sidewalk by a right turn lane for cars. I took a chance and ran in front of a car that was in the turn lane, causing the driver to slam on her brakes and yell a curse at me, but I had no time to respond to her insults.

On the corner of Broadway and Columbus was a strip club named El Cid. I ran past it, then past a restaurant named Edna's English Fish & Chips, and then I stopped in front of a restaurant named Little Joe's. There was a line of people on the sidewalk waiting to be seated at Little Joe's. With the line of people added to the Saturday night throngs, I lost sight of The White Rabbit.

I scanned the area, looking for white hair and a gray overcoat. Suddenly The White Rabbit dashed out of the crowd and crossed the street mid-block. Once on the other side of Columbus Avenue he ducked into a doorway one store front from the triangular corner formed by the intersection of Columbus and Grant Avenues, which ran at an angle to one another. Throwing caution to the wind, I ran across Columbus Avenue mid-block, reached the door and entered a place called Gulliver's. It was a crowded bar with a blues band playing on a stage to my right.

In the back of the room I saw The White Rabbit at the top of a stairway that led to a glass door. The door was in a row of windows that were high on the back wall, through which people could be seen as they walked along a sidewalk. The White Rabbit opened the door and exited Gulliver's.

When I reached the top of the stairs, I saw that the door led out onto Grant Avenue, which was two meters higher than Columbus Avenue on the backside of Gulliver's. Through the door I saw The White Rabbit enter a bar across the street.

I exited Gulliver's and crossed Grant Avenue to the bar. In the front window a neon beer sign glowed brightly and the name,

Saloon was painted in gold leaf on the window. Next to the door a hand lettered sign was posted that read, The Door Slammers.

Sitting on a barstool in the doorway was a man with dark hair and beard collecting a cover charge. "Two bucks," he said as I approached the door. I paid him and he said, "Give me your hand," in what I thought was an odd version of a New York accent. I held out my hand and he took the cap off of a writing instrument with Sharpie printed on its barrel. With it he made one tiny, black dot on the back of my hand. "Okay, you can go in now," he said.

"Are you from New York?" I asked to verify my guess.

"No. I was born and raised in this neighborhood," he answered.

Then it dawned on me; he was speaking with the extinct San Francisco accent, which bore a slight similarity to a New York accent. My professor had recordings of the last surviving speakers and occasionally gave lectures at sociolinguistics seminars on the accent. We spent a week on it in her class and I was amazed at my luck to hear it spoken by a native speaker. But I had no time to ponder this rarity as I entered an ancient room, crowded with dancers and blaring, amplified blues music.

The song the band was playing came to an end while I negotiated my way through the crowd. As I reached the bar, the band leader advised those in attendance to, "Start drinking triples until you're seeing double and forgetting you're single." Then he introduced the next song, "Okay, now we're going to get your bacon shakin'." The band started up again and the din refilled the room.

Behind the bar was a gray haired bartender wearing a black top hat. As I inched my way through the crowd, I heard someone call my name. I looked around and someone else called my name. *What is going on?* I wondered. Then someone else called out my name and the bartender went to where he stood at the bar. *Oh! The bartender is also named John*, I realized. I made my way to the bar and called out, "John!"

The bartender looked at me, then came to where I stood. "Have you seen The White Rabbit?" I asked loudly to be heard over the music.

"Do you want a drink?" he responded, just as loudly.

"I will take a San Miguel," I ordered a beer that I knew.

"The beers we carry are listed there," John pointed to a hand let-tered sign posted on the backbar, then turned to my left and walked toward the short end of the bar at the front of the room. There, in a cul-de-sac formed by the short end of the bar, the right wall and the front wall, stood The White Rabbit. He was trapped.

I started to move in his direction when I bumped into a tall, grim faced man wearing a long, black leather coat. "Watch your-self, pal," he said, in an intimidating manner.

I excused myself and tried to squeeze between him and an-other male customer who wore a knee length brocade coat, black knee boots and a top hat. They blocked my view for a moment and when I was finally able to get past them I saw The White Rabbit slip through the door and escape out onto Grant Avenue.

Damn!

Grant Avenue
Chapter 6

I RAN OUT ONTO GRANT AVENUE, BUT THERE WAS NO SIGN OF The White Rabbit. *Damn! I will never catch him.* A sense of defeat settled over me. *I can't give up now, I hope Sarah will understand.*

I began walking slowly up hill. Next to the Saloon I encountered a restaurant named La Pantera. *Maybe he went in there*, I thought, without much enthusiasm. I opened the door to a restaurant filled with diners. A man in a sport coat greeted me, then invited me to eat, "It's family style, you won't be eating alone," he said in accented English, gesturing to the picnic tables that filled the room.

"I am not hungry, I am looking for a man called The White Rabbit, is he here?"

"No sir. This is a nice place, that man isn't allowed in here," he answered, with a sour look on his face.

His response made me feel it was a safe bet that The White Rabbit wasn't in the room. I thanked him, turned to the street and on the opposing corner saw a brightly lit cafe. *Maybe he is there*, I thought, as I crossed the street.

Cafe Trieste was painted in yellow, red and black enamel on the large, plate glass window of the cafe. As I entered the smell of coffee made me realize I could use a pick-me-up. I got into the line and stood with my back to the counter so I could survey the room. *This is so inconvenient compared with auto-serve*, I thought, as the line inched forward.

The counter and the work space behind it took up a good deal of the front of the cafe, so most of the tables were in the back. The tables were filled with people who sat smoking cigarettes and drinking coffee, beer, and wine. Intense conversations were going on throughout the room. A cloud of tobacco smoke hung in the air.

Covering most of the back wall was a mural of a fishing village, presumably Trieste. Near where I stood five two-tops were grouped together to form one long table. The chairs around this group of tables were filled by an assortment of people. Against the back wall, under the mural, near an old, upright piano, was a smaller table occupied by a smaller group of people. A heated argument was in progress between the two groups.

When the argument seemed to be reaching culmination, a man sitting with the small group pointed at a man sitting with the large group and, in a booming voice that filled the room, called him a Left Leaning Leninite. At that point the man so accused stood. He was tall and thin, wore a long, olive drab coat and had a large, reddish brown, droopy mustache. He raised a finger in the air and loudly proclaimed, "Stephen, you know damn well that I'm a Stalinist till death!" Then he launched into a series of proclamations in a resonate voice. Meanwhile, a petite woman seated next to him, wearing a flowered dress with her hair piled high on her head, reached up, grabbed his coat and tugged on it. "Enough Jack, sit down," she said. Jack the Stalinist made a final choice comment to his grinning tormentor, then abruptly sat, turned to the woman and they began a whispered conversation.

I turned from this scene and looked directly across from where I stood. Four small tables lined the window that ran along Grant Avenue. At the end of this row of tables, at the boundary between the front and back portions of the room, was a telephone booth. I had never seen one, except in old movies, so I was thrilled when the phone inside of it rang. It rang a second time. When it rang for a third time, a man sitting in a chair adjacent to the booth stood, leaned into the booth and picked up the handset. "Yeah, he's here," I heard him say. He held the handset high, looked toward the front of the room and yelled to a man sitting at a table near the front door, "Hey Kim, it's for you." Then he let the handset dangle by its cord and resumed his seat.

Kim, who had an athletic build, short, reddish hair and was

wearing short pants and a T-shirt, got up from his chair, walked to the phone booth, then entered it and closed the door.

The line I was standing in moved forward and I soon had a cup of expresso in hand. I turned from the counter to locate a seat. I felt that I should sit where I could keep an eye on the door, in case The White Rabbit was present and tried to escape. Next to me was a large, round table where a portly man with brown hair sat by himself, writing on a pad of paper. I gathered the nerve to ask him if I could share his table. He looked up, gave me a slightly annoyed look, then replied, "Yeah, sure. It's a free country." Then he went back to writing.

I took a seat and sipped my coffee. "Excuse me," emboldened by my predicament, I dared to bother him again.

"Yes?" He replied curtly, without looking up from his writing.

"Do you know a man called The White Rabbit?"

He looked up, then replied, "Yes, I know him. Don't much care for him, but I know him."

"So... he borrowed something from me and I want it back," I explained. "Have you seen him tonight?"

"So far as I know, The White Rabbit doesn't borrow anything. But as a matter of fact I have seen him. Just a few moments ago I stopped writing to collect my thoughts. While I was gazing out the window I happen to see him walking up Grant Avenue. I assume he was going to Ben's Poster Matt to borrow money, so to speak, from Ben. But to be honest, I didn't give it much thought."

I picked up my demitasse and drained it. "Thanks! I have to go." I stood and pulled the door open.

As I exited the cafe I heard him say, "Come again when you can stay longer," in a sarcastic tone of voice.

Kitty-corner from the Trieste was a shop with a sign that read, Ben's Poster Matt. I crossed the street and entered a cluttered shop that was filled with bins containing old record albums with colorful cardboard sleeves. Posters covered the walls and the ceiling. To my left was a darkened nook where posters glowed in unnaturally bright colors under an ultra-violet light. In front of me was a counter, behind which stood a bearded man wearing a Greek fisherman's cap. He was leaning against the counter top reading a newspaper. He continued reading for a moment after I entered, then looked up from his paper. "What can I do for you?" he asked.

I was about to answer his question when my attention was diverted by movement above and behind him. I looked up and perched on a narrow ledge above him was the biggest cat I have ever seen. And not just big, but fat too.

He turned and looked up to see what was distracting me. "Kitty-kitty, come down here," he said emphatically. The cat didn't move a muscle, other than to yawn expansively. His mouth must have been dry, because when he finished his yawn his upper lip got stuck on his teeth, leaving them exposed in what appeared to be a fiendish grin.

"Cats are very independent creatures," the bearded man said, as a way to explain his lack of control over the animal.

"What is its name?" I asked, thinking that may be the key to getting the cat to come down.

He gave me a perplexed look, then replied, "Kitty-kitty."

"Oh," I said, thinking that this man wasn't very creative when it came to naming his pet. Then I asked the question I'd come to ask, "I am looking for a man they call The White Rabbit. Have you seen him?"

"Hmm... Now that you mention it, I did see him. Just a moment ago. I looked up from my paper as he walked by. He was heading up the street, seemed to be in a hurry. There's a show at The Savoy Tivoli tonight, maybe that's where he was going."

"Thank you." With my spirits picking up I left and started to walk briskly up Grant Avenue. But my progress was soon halted when a shop across the street named Middle Earth caught my attention. It had an assortment of women's clothes on display in the window, but what had caught my attention was the unusual typeface the sign painter used. *Now that's an adventurous typeface, ugly, but adventurous.* And the name Middle Earth rang a bell, though I was unable to place it. *I must stay focused,* I thought, and continued walking up Grant Avenue.

As I walked I noticed that Grant Avenue looked oddly narrow. I had noticed the same thing on Broadway, but was too over-

come by the frenetic street activity to do more than take notice. Now, in a calmer setting, I was able to stop and ponder the mystery. The simple explanation soon occurred to me; the cars parked along each curb made the street seem narrower. I congratulated myself for solving the mystery.

I started to move on, but only made a few paces of progress before a handwritten sign, that was hung in the window of a shop across the street, caught my eye. It appeared to be written in chalk on a small, wooden framed piece of slate. The writing read, Live Worms. *What kind of a shop could make a go of it selling worms?* I looked at the rest of the store front, which had a large sign that read, Figoni Hardware. *Why would a hardware store sell worms? Fishing bait? But who would go fishing? There are no fish in the bay, not that are edible. But if it is 1979 maybe people were still fishing in the bay in those days... These days?*

With one mystery solved and a second to ponder, I continued on my way, my thoughts momentarily disrupted by blues music blaring from two bars across the street.

Next I crossed Green Street, where a shop called East West Leather stood on the corner. I naturally assumed it was a faux leather shop, but as I passed it an unusual and pleasant fragrance wafted out the door, reminding me of something from childhood. *Damn!* I thought, realizing that this was a real leather shop filled with a c.e.o.'s ransom in cow leather. I know that they still sell real leather in a convenience store downtown, but that shop primarily sells pigskin suede. Cow leather has to be special ordered. And the door of this shop stood wide open. If I had any lingering doubts as to whether I was indeed in 1979, those doubts now faded.

As I continued up Grant Avenue my progress was arrested by yet another store front. The sign above this one read, The Schlock Shop. The window was filled with very old, everyday things. Some were so old I had no idea what they could have been used for and most were covered with a layer of dust. I was reluctant to open the door, but I overcame my reluctance and did so, then leaned through the doorway. A gnarled old man with a bristling salt-and-pepper mustache sat behind the counter. He was wearing a hat and the shelves behind him were filled with hats, stacked one upon another. Above him an antique, red fireman's hat was suspended by thin, nylon filaments. The rest of the small shop was so jam packed that it seemed no space was left empty. I entered and asked, "May I look around?"

"Of course. Be my guest," the old man replied.

I began looking in the glass display cases at things I felt belonged in a museum. One thing in particular stood out; what appeared to be a folded piece of parchment. *That must be extremely old.* The part that was visible had names handwritten in black ink with an oblique pen nib. An *X* or similar mark was next to each name. I turned from the case, "Is this parchment?" I asked the shopkeeper.

He craned his neck, rose slightly, then settled back into his chair. "Yes, that's an indentured servants manifest. It's dated 1697."

"May I see it?" I asked.

"No. It's not for sale," he replied.

"But I just want to see it."

"The case is glass, you can see it," he pointed out the obvious.

"But it is folded, I want to see the rest of it," I pleaded.

"Look, do you want to buy a hat? Because I don't have time to run around opening cases for looky-loos," he said in an agitated tone of voice.

His tone offended me so, in a somewhat self-righteous tone, I replied, "Do not have the time? You are just sitting there doing nothing."

"Get the hell out of my shop," he yelled at me and stood, as if he might come out from behind the counter. Old man or not, I didn't want to get into an altercation, so I quickly exited the shop.

Resuming my walk I notice another shop next door. Its sign read, The Scene. It was darkened and appeared to be closed. Displayed in the window was a small painting on a small easel. It was an amateurish portrait of the same disagreeable old man I just encountered in The Schlock Shop. In it he was striking a heroic pose in a fireman's hat. *I'll bet that's a self portrait...*

"Hey! El Futuro, where you going?" A high pitched, feminine voice broke the spell cast by the store front. "We wondered where you went."

I turned to see Holly and Ruben walking toward me. "I went to chase The White Rabbit. I heard he might be at The

Savoy Tivoli," I told them. "I think it is up this way."

"Yup, that's where we're going," Holly replied. "You're almost there, come with us." As we walked, Holly's high heels click-clacked on the sidewalk. It was a sound unfamiliar to me, with a mildly erotic quality. She pointed across the street to a bay window that overhung Grant Avenue. "That's where I live," she said. "And I work at good old Beaumont McGillicuddy's. You passed it back there in the last block," she gestured over her shoulder. "It's a used clothing shop," she explained, then added, "I have an easy commute."

Ahead I saw a yellow sign mounted perpendicular to a building that read, The Savoy Tivoli. The sign was written in raised, wooden letters in a red and black art nouveau typeface which incorporated stylized animals in its design. It was on the same side of the street we were walking. *Good, it's close,* I was thinking, when Ruben started for the other side of the street.

"Where are you going? The Savoy Tivoli is right here," I said, pointing at the sign.

"I know, John, but we're going to the S&S market first to buy Miller High Life. They carry it at the Savoy so they'll think we bought it there. That'll save us a buck or so," Ruben explained our detour.

We crossed the street, then entered a brightly lit little store with narrow aisles and well stocked shelves. An Asian store clerk stood behind the counter, where a line of people were buying beer, cigarettes and other assorted items. I followed Ruben and Holly to the back of the store where there was a row of refrigerators with glass doors. Ruben opened a door and handed me a clear glass bottle of beer with a red, white and gold label. Then he took out two more of the same bottles and we got into the check-out-line. *This is so inconvenient compared to auto-check-out,* I thought, as Ruben paid for his beers.

When it was my turn to pay, the clerk said, "Fifty cents."

That is almost free. I placed a dollar bill on the counter. *Should I leave a tip? Ruben didn't.* I put the two coins I received in change into my pocket.

"Here, let me carry them in my purse," Holly said. Ruben and I both handed her our beers, which she buried in her purse.

The Savoy Tivoli
Chapter 7

Afloor had a faux stone facade that was painted white with red
and green trim. The establishment was split into two parts; on
the right side there was a door and two small, arched windows,
through which a barroom could be partially seen. On the left
side was an open front restaurant recessed into the building.
The open front gave the restaurant the look and feel of a patio.
We entered on the patio side by climbing two steps through a
gap in a low wall that separated it from the sidewalk.

"Blondie and the Ramones played here a couple of years
ago," Holly turned to tell me as she stepped onto the patio level.
It must have been my uncomprehending stare that caused her
to add, "Not on the same night… But still."

On our way through the patio I noticed a large, slate
menu, handwritten in chalk, against the left wall at the front
near the sidewalk. It had a wooden frame with the legend
"Why can't people see that patience and leisure are intertwined?" hand painted in an Art Nouveau script. Holly must
have noticed that I was reading the sign because she laughed
and said, "That sign means you better expect slow service."

I followed her and Ruben past a small bar, where we came
to a wall of sliding wooden doors inset with plate glass panels
that separated the interior room from the patio. Since it was a
warm night, the doors were slid open, allowing air to circulate.
We entered the interior room through a gap in the sliding doors

and made our way through a crowd of people. At the back of this interior space we got into a short line that formed outside of a small doorway. The door was closed and a muted din came from within. Whenever the door was opened to allow a patron to enter or exit, the muted din became noticeably louder.

As we waited I looked around the room, which was filled with tables where patrons drank and dined. There was also a line of three support columns, the first of which was in the patio, the second and third were in the interior room. Fake palm fronds, fashioned out of sheet metal, were attached around their tops. At the base of the center column was a fake pond. *This place wasn't designed by an algorithm,* I thought idly, as the line moved forward.

"Hey, Ruben, Holly." I turned from examining the decor to see who was greeting my new friends. It was a tall man with brown hair, who stood at the door we were about to pass through. Next to him stood a pretty blond woman.

"Hi, Jerry, hi Olga," Holly said. "This is our new friend, El Futuro, he's from the future. We met him at the Mab," Holly said, gesturing to me.

"Pleased to meet you, El Futuro," Olga said with a smile.

"Just go on in, Holly," Jerry said, with an English accent.

"Gee, thanks, Jerry."

Jerry opened the door for Holly, allowing the music to blare from the hallway.

After Ruben was also given a free pass, Jerry said to me, "Two bucks."

I paid him, then entered a narrow hallway where I was immediately hit by a blast of heat, humidity and loud music. Just ahead of me Holly stopped at a doorway on our left and yelled, "Hey, Patrick, hot enough for you?"

"Thanks, Holly. It's roasting in here," a voice answered from within.

Holly turned to me and, speaking loudly to be heard over the music, explained, "That's one of my neighbors, Patrick. He lives upstairs with his girlfriend in the Tivoli Towers."

As I passed the door I looked into a cramped room that contained a large stove and lots of pots and pans. Bending over the stove was a man in a white coat with curly brown hair and a goatee. He was stirring something in a pan as sweat dripped from his forehead. *That is inhumane and not terribly hygienic,* I thought, never having seen a human chef.

We continued down the narrow hallway that opened into a room where a low stage abutted the back and left walls. On either side of the stage were two large, matched angels made from some sort of cast metal. There was standing room in the front and off to the right side of the stage. Just to our right was a small service bar against the wall. On the stage a band was playing music at great volume while thrashing about with their instruments. The lead singer was a tall, thin man with short, dark, spiky hair and exaggerated eye makeup. He held a microphone in his hands as he sang, "Johnny you're too bad... "

"Hi, Christine. Here to see The Offs?" Holly said loudly to a brunette who walked toward us, gracefully balanced on stiletto heels. Her hair was cut short and she was dressed in an iridescent, pink plastic rain coat which she wore unbuttoned, revealing a white shirt and pencil thin black pants.

"Of course, it's about the only time I can keep an eye on Billy," she laughed.

Ruben turned to me and leaned in close. "She's so hot. She looks like Bianca Jagger," he said loudly into my ear, causing me to recoil in pain.

I don't know who Bianca Jagger is, but this woman is beautiful and very well dressed, I thought, as I looked away from her to scan the room for The White Rabbit.

Although the music was louder than suited my taste, it was good, with a sort of lilting, in-and-out quality to it. "Here," Holly said, as she bumped her hand into mine. I looked down and saw she was holding the bottle of beer I'd bought across the street. "Don't let the bartender see you open it," she cautioned, with a toss of her head in the direction of the service bar.

"Thanks," I said, taking the bottle. I watched as she held her bottle low and out of sight, grabbed the cap and twisted it off, then dropped the cap on the floor. I followed her lead and soon tipped my head back for a large gulp. After swallowing my beer I

complained loudly, "It is hot in here. And smoky, too."

She nodded as she took another gulp of her beer.

"Holly, Ruben... El Futuro," a male voice was projected loudly from behind us.

I turned to see Hugh the photographer, wrestling his camera into a more comfortable position.

"Tired of photographing the Mutants, Hugh?" Holly asked.

"No, I got plenty of shots and they're almost done. But The Offs just got back from New York and I've heard rumors that they're moving there. I figured I'd better come up here and shoot a couple rolls of them, then double back to The Mab to photograph The Go-Go's. The Units are playing between the Mutants' and The Go-Go's and I just photographed them and The Liars over in Berkeley at Aitos last Tuesday anyways."

"That's a complicated life you lead, Hugh," Ruby said loudly, as she and Ivey walked up behind Hugh.

"I guess you had the same idea as me, huh, Ruby?" Hugh replied.

"Yeah. I want to get some shots of The Offs before I have to photograph The Go-Go's for *Slash,* if I want to get paid," Ruby said.

The room wasn't just hot and loud, it was also very smokey. And conversation was difficult, because every word had to be shouted to be heard. Up near the stage, people were leaping up and down. The room was much smaller than the Mabuhay, so I couldn't get far enough away from the leaping people for comfort. Besides that, I couldn't see the group on stage. Then I remembered my theory about why people were doing this sort of dance, if it was a dance. As my space became encroached by a tall fellow who suddenly began jumping vigorously along with the crowd. I joined in and began jumping up and down myself. By doing so I was able to catch sporadic glimpses of the group on stage. On top of that, while I was airborne my concern about the tall fellow stomping on my foot was greatly reduced. I began to enjoy the sensation, it felt almost like flying. But then I realized that I had to take a leak again. "I need to use the restroom," I yelled to Holly.

She turned and nodded at me.

Once outside I encountered Olga, who was watching the door. "Olga, I have to use the restroom. Where is it?" I asked.

She jerked her thumb over her shoulder toward a passageway, "Go into the main barroom, turn left and walk down the hallway, it'll be the door on your right."

After passing through the passageway Olga indicated, I came to the main barroom. Compared with the patio, this one was dimly lit and the bar was much longer. Above the back bar was a backlit line of over thirty art deco glass-globe light fixtures, each of a different design. *Oh my god! Those are museum pieces. They are worth a fortune.* I began to fantasize about how they could be used, but my needs were becoming more urgent and I turned away to find the men's room.

I walked past a row of four wooden booths that were painted dark-cadmium red, in which couples sat drinking and talking. A scruffy man with short, gray hair sat in the last booth, with a clutter of art supplies arrayed on his table. Though he had a wide assortment of art materials to choose from, he chose to work with a plain No. 2 graphite pencil on a sheet of illustration board. I stopped for a moment to see what he was drawing, but it was impossible to tell because the pencil marks were layered·one upon another until the illustration board was almost uniformly graphite gray. He stopped his drawing to look over his shoulder at me.

"What are you drawing?" I asked.

"Mind your own business!" he snapped.

I quickly moved on, thinking, *that is the most extreme case of an artist over-working a piece that I have ever seen.*

Finally I came to a short, dead end hallway. The door at the end of it was marked Women. Another door, on the right side, was marked Men. It opened and Jerry walked out. He nodded at me as he passed me in the hallway.

I entered a restroom that smelled strongly of disinfectant and was painted a lurid salmon pink. I walked up to a urinal and unzipped my fly. I noticed that the paint on the walls was a heavy type of enamel that I was unfamiliar with. I reached up and touched it. *This stuff will last forever,* was my professional opinion. *That is too bad,* was my professional critique of the color choice. As I was relieving myself I had nothing to look at other than the wall directly in front of me. On it someone had written,

"Drugs may be the road to nowhere, but at least it's the scenic route." I chuckled at the 20ᵗʰ century humor, as two men emerged from a stall in the back of the room.

"That's good stuff. Where'd you get it?" one man asked the other.

His companion sniffed loudly, then replied, "From that guy Eric. I met him when he worked at Flax Art Supplies. He has that hot Asian girlfriend."

"Oh yeah, I know them. Her name is Dian and she is gorgeous. But I heard they broke up."

"No, I've seen them together recently. Let's get a beer."

The two men left the restroom as I was washing my hands. I noted that neither of them washed theirs. When I was finished I left the restroom and walked back down the hallway.

My beer was getting low and it was already warm, plus it had become foamy, so I stopped at the long bar where I took an empty barstool. As I waited for the bartender to finish with a customer, I looked at the row of light fixtures above the back bar. *Each of those could be used as the center piece for an entire room*, I thought.

"Hey Tony!" a customer called out. The bartender went to where the customer stood at the bar.

When that customer had a beer in front of him I called out, "Hey Tony!" The bartender, a young man with short, dark hair, came to where I sat. I ordered another Miller, then waited as he got one out of the refrigerator from behind the bar. I took a last swig of my beer, put the near empty bottle on the bar and looked around the room. The White Rabbit wasn't present.

I paid the bartender with a twenty, received my change, then got up and walked to the door where Jerry and Olga stood watch. Jerry was introducing two blond women who were dressed in black leather, to a stout, balding man who wore a black, leather jacket and blue jeans.

"Go on in, El Futuro," Olga said.

"Howie, this is Heidi and this is Jeorgia," was the last thing I heard Jerry say before Olga pulled the door open and loud music drowned out everything else.

Just as I reached the back room the music stopped. The singer, who was standing at the front of the stage, growled a few things into the microphone. Due to bad acoustics I couldn't make out what he said, but a number of people laughed and one man yelled out, "Tell us more, Don!"

The singer replied, "Don't make me come down there to your level and make a man out of you," which caused more laughter to ripple through the audience.

"Hey, El Futuro." Holly greeted me, as she approached me from the left side of the room. "This is Hank," she said, introducing me to a tall woman with short dark hair who walked beside her. "Hank, this is El Futuro." I shook Hank's hand as Holly explained, "Hank is a clothing designer. My friend Camille and I are starting a business making punk clothes, we're going to call it Holl-Cam Enterprises. Ruben came up with the name. Hank was telling me how to file a Fictitious Name Statement. You still nursing that beer from the S&S?"

I looked down at the bottle in my hand, "No, I just bought it at the bar in the main barroom."

"Oh, so that's what took you so long. Anybody we know out there?"

"How would I know?" I replied. At this point the band started up again. I smiled and nodded at Hank, in lieu of a comment, and she walked away to stand at the back of the room next to the right side of the stage.

I looked around to see if I could spot The White Rabbit. As I scanned the crowd my eyes fell upon a tall young woman standing against the left wall. She had short brown, wavy hair, wore heavy black framed eye glasses with no make-up, a sweat shirt with a short skirt and black canvas shoes. *That may be the most attractive woman I have ever seen.* As I studied her she looked at me and I quickly averted my gaze.

Due to the cloud of tobacco smoke, the heat and humidity, and the blaring music, I began to feel nauseous. A few minutes later I decided to go outside for relief. I looked around the room and saw that Holly and Ruben had wandered away and were now standing up front, near the stage. *They won't miss me, I need to get out of here.* I walked back down the narrow hallway and through the door. "I have to get some air," I explained to Olga, as I passed her on my way out.

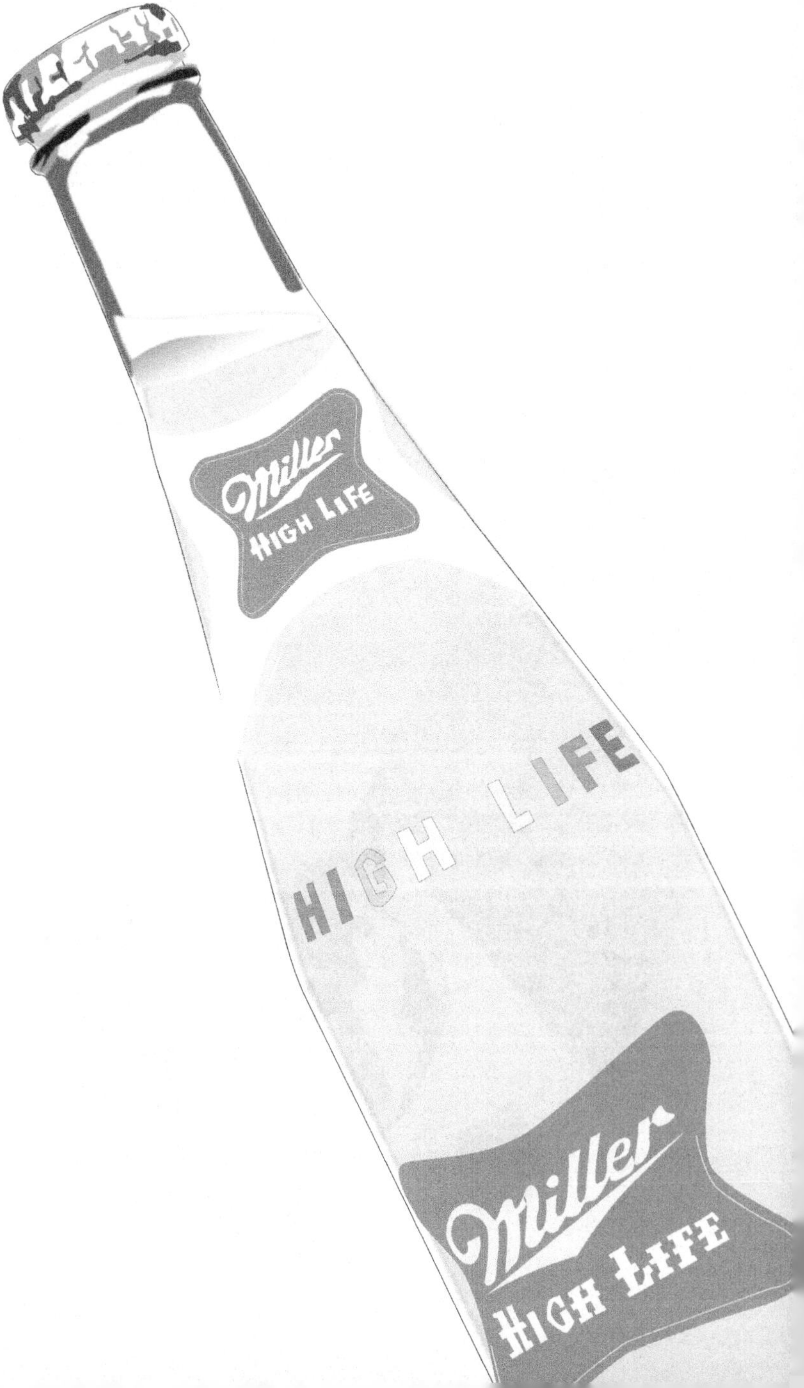
Miller
HIGH LIFE
HIGH LIFE
Miller
HIGH LIFE

The Patio
Chapter 8

ONCE ON THE PATIO I FELT MUCH BETTER. I LOOKED FOR a place to sit and saw a couple leaving a table. It was at the front of the patio, near the sidewalk, under the large, slate menu I saw as we entered. As soon as they left I took a seat there and sat with my back to the wall, giving me an unobstructed view of the patio and Grant Avenue. As I sat drinking my beer and watching people come and go, I noticed that my ears were ringing. Soon a waiter, who was a tall, thin black man wearing a leopard print mini-skirt came to bus the table. Remembering what Holly said about the slow service, I ordered another beer before I finished the one in my hand.

As the waiter walked away I relaxed and took a gulp of beer. *This is much better than that hot, cramped, smoky little room.* I took a deep breath and, detecting an objectionable odor, I turned my head and sniffed the sleeve of my jacket. It reeked of tobacco smoke.

Then my attention was drawn to the street activity. The sidewalk in front of the Savoy Tivoli swirled with Saturday night revelers. Out of the crowd, the odd fellow that Mark the doorman ejected from the Mabuhay, came walking up the sidewalk. He stopped in front of my table and looked at me. "Have we met?" he asked.

"No. I saw you at the Mabuhay, briefly," I replied diplomatically.

"Oh, of course. You were with Holly and Ivey and the gang. Sorry about my quick exit, didn't mean to be rude, but it was unavoidable. The doorman doesn't like me for some reason. Ah well, as grandmama says, 'Fuck'em if they can't take a joke.' Pardon my French, but he rubs me the wrong way."

"No offense taken," again I tried my best to be diplomatic with someone who was beginning to make me uncomfortable.

He climbed gracelessly over the low wall from the sidewalk into the patio, pulling his ascot askew as he did. "My name is Sven," he gasped his introduction, sweating from exertion. "I'm from New Jersey. Not *Jersey*, but *New Jersey*." He said, pronouncing *New Jersey* very clearly and precisely, as if he was trying to impress me. "May I join you?" he asked, as he seated himself at my table.

"Well... sure," I replied, having been left no other choice. *The u-bees do things differently,* I found comfort in Sarah's words.

Sven settled in, then quickly launched into a series of proclamations about art, fashion and culture. At one point he stopped to say, "I tell you all this because I sense that you're contemporary. Very few people are contemporary. I assume you are able to appreciate what I have to say, most people cannot."

"Actually I am not contemporary," I corrected him, "I am from the future."

My comment seemed to confuse him. "Oh yes, the future. So am I. In fact... "

"No, I mean I am from the future. I live in the year 2063. That is eighty-four years in your future," I explained.

"Uh... what? Do you have a time machine?" Sven struggled to comprehend my statement.

"No. It just sort of happened. I was chasing The White Rabbit up a dark stairwell in a bar called The Rabbit Hole and there... here I was, back in 1979." None of this seemed to help. In fact now he was the one acting uncomfortable.

He turned his head to scan the patio. "Holly, Ivey," he exclaimed, seemingly relieved to have a distraction. I turned my head and saw Holly and Ivey walking toward our table.

"Hi, El Futuro, I wondered where you went. Hi Sven. I didn't know you two knew each other," Holly said, smiling.

"'El Futuro', is that what they call you?" Sven asked me.

"Yes, some people. But they just started calling me that tonight," I explained, as Holly and Ivey joined us at the table and the waiter showed up with my beer.

After I paid for my drink, the waiter turned to Sven, who was the only member of our group without a drink. Sven turned to me, "Pardon me for asking, El Futuro, but could you see your way clear to spot me a drink? I seem to be financially embarrassed; walked out of the house without a dime in my pocket." He stopped for a moment, bent his head down and chuckled. Then he continued, "Grandmama is a bit forgetful herself. I guess it runs in the family."

"Yeah, sure. What would you like?" With my pocket stuffed with cash and considering how little drinks cost in this time period, I was feeling generous.

"Well, old man, I'd like a Brandy Alexander." He looked at the waiter, "Have the bartender make it with Courvoisier, would you dearie?"

"But of course," the waiter replied, in a put-on snooty accent, then turned and walked toward the small bar on the other side of the patio.

"Just can't get good help these days, El Futuro. It's getting to be a real problem for Grandmama," Sven sniffed, readjusting his ascot as he did.

"And you can pick your nose, but you can't pick your table mates," Ivey said, as she rose from her chair. "I'm going to the S&S for smokes. Anybody want anything?"

"Actually, I could use a pack of Marlboros," Sven said, handing over a one dollar bill.

Ivey took the bill, then began to leave when Sven stopped her. "And Ivey... don't forget my change," he said, speaking in a musical tone of voice.

"I'll be right back," she said, giving Sven a look of exasperation, before turning and walking toward the other side of the street.

A moment later Hugh and Ruby walked out onto the patio and stopped at our table for a moment. "The Offs are done. I think I got some great shots of Don, he's so photogenic," Ruby said, then asked, "Where's Ivey?"

"She went to get cigarettes at the S&S," Holly replied.

"Oh well, tell her I'm at the Mab, if I don't see her there, I'll see her at home."

"Okay, Ruby, I'll tell her."

"See you guys," Hugh said, as he and Ruby exited the patio and turned left onto Grant Avenue, heading back toward the Mabuhay.

A few minutes later Ivey returned and tossed a pack of cigarettes and two coins on the table in front of Sven. Then she sat down, lit a cigarette and glanced around the patio. "Hey, Snuky," Ivey said loudly to a stocky black man, with a mop of hair tied on top of his head, who had just entered the patio from the street.

Snuky turned his head, smiled, then said, "Hey, Ivey. Are The Offs still playing?"

"Just finished," she answered.

"Shit. Can I join you guys?"

"Sure, Snuky. Take a load off," Ivey said. She took another drag on her cigarette, then asked, "Want a calendar? Hot off the presses," she offered him her stack.

"Thanks Ivey," Snuky took one off the top, folded it and jammed it into his hip pocket. "Let me get a beer," he said, then turned and walked to the bar behind him.

At this point I noticed that the young woman I had admired in the back room had taken a seat at a table to my left. I watched as she ordered from the waiter. In better light I could now see that her skin was very pale, as if she rarely went out during the day. She also had several beauty marks, which increased the loveliness of her face. *She is so beautiful.* When she finished ordering, she turned her head and looked directly at me. I quickly looked away.

"So when do The Liars start?" Snuky asked, as he pulled up a chair at a table adjacent to ours.

"Probably twenty minutes," Ivey answered, scooting her chair around slightly to speak with Snuky. "Were you at the Mab? I didn't see you there."

"Yeah. I got there late, just caught the Mutants' last three songs. But I see them all the time anyway, we're working on a project together. I hoped I could catch the end of The Offs' set before The Liars. I love The Offs, but they're playing at the Deaf Club next week, so I'll catch them there. I heard they had a great time in New York, so who knows how long before they move there."

As Snuky was finishing his sentence, Magdeline and Eva walked in from the street. "I take it The Offs are done. You mind, Snuky?" Eva asked, as she pulled out a chair from Snuky's table. Snuky gestured at the chair with an opened palm and both Eva and Magdeline took seats at his table. "When do The Liars start?" Magdeline asked.

"Twenty minutes," Snuky answered, as Ruben also took a seat at his table. I noticed that half of Ruben's mustache was missing.

"Ladies, gentlemen... Sven," Ruben greeted those present. "Snuky, want a postcard? Free sample from the president of Fast, Cheap & Easy Graphics," he said, pulling a small deck of cards, held together by a rubber band, from the inside pocket of his sport coat.

"Sure," Snuky said, taking the deck and removing the rubber band. He sorted through them and finally decided on one. Then he put the rubber band around the remaining cards and returned them to Ruben.

"Let me see which one you took, it's how we do our test marketing." Snuky showed Ruben the card he chose. "Ah... excellent choice," Ruben said, in a dramatic tone of voice. Next he started to offer his cards to Magdeline and Eva, but they were in a discussion, so he turned to me, "Here, John, take one. I'm interested in how posterity will judge my work," he said, handing me the cards.

I quickly looked through the deck of stiff, slightly off rectangles, looking as if they had been cut by hand. The designs included images with phrases such as: Why Not Save His Sperm, I Dreamed That My Grandmother Bit Me, One Vote, and Can Wet Dreams Cause VD? I looked through several others before deciding on one with a crude depiction of the American flag painted in yellow and blue with multi-colored stars that read, Fat Free America. I showed it to him, to which he responded, "Ah... excellent choice," in a dramatic tone of voice which, apparently, was his stock response.

"How are these produced?" I asked, as I took a last swig of my beer and put the empty bottle in the center of our small table.

"Well, they're mostly collage with some painting and drawing. I do the original artwork on pieces of cardboard or whatever's handy. Then I photocopy them, four-up, on a color Xerox machine. Then I photo mount eight of the Xerox prints on a large sheet of Hammermill index card stock and finally I cut them up on a paper cutter, then stamp the backs with my rubber stamp."

"They're not art, they're Nart," Ivey interjected.

I turned the card over and saw that Fast, Cheap & Easy Graphics was unevenly printed on the back in blue ink. "That's a lot of work. Does anybody buy them?" I asked, as I picked up my full bottle of beer.

"Yeah. I sell them a number of places here in the city: Sh-Boom on Brady Alley off Market Street, The Punk Compound on 16th Street in the Mission, The Postcard Palace in North Beach on Columbus, and Poor Taste, which is just up the street on the corner of Grant and Filbert."

"I love Poor Taste," Holly said. "John Becker's such a nice man."

"Yeah, John's cool. And he offered me a job at Poor Taste if I ever move across the bay," Ruben agreed. "John's the owner of Poor Taste," he explained to me, "among other things, like collectibles, hats and used books, he sells postcards, including mine. And I also sell them over in Berkeley, where I live, and on College Avenue in North Oakland."

Poor Taste, where have I heard that name before?

"I saw your cards at Hot Flash up in The Castro last month," Snuky said.

"Oh yeah, that's one of my best outlets. I just delivered a big order to them last Tuesday on my day off. I also made a sale to Fiorucci in New York while I was there last month," Ruben said.

"Tuesday? What was the mood in the Castro?" Snuky asked.

"Pretty bleak. The clerk I delivered the cards to said there was going to be a demonstration on Castro that night," Ruben answered. "He advised me to avoid it."

"Yeah, but I heard it was peaceful. Everyone was expecting the worst after Monday night," Snuky said.

"Twinkies, can you believe it? Dan White got away with murder," Ivey added. "I hear there's going to be several punk benefits for the legal and medical fees for the victims of the police riot. They're in the planning stage now. They'll be listed in my calendar as soon as I get the details."

"Yeah, and now we got that bitch Feinstein as mayor. I was there when she shut down a Sunday afternoon punk show at the Gay Community Center because she got complaints from little old ladies in mink stoles who used to walk by on their way to the Sunday afternoon opera rehearsals," Ruben said in an angry tone.

"Oh Ivey," Holly interrupted, "Ruby said to tell you she went back to the Mab with Hugh."

"Thanks Holly," Ivey replied.

"Do you make a living selling your postcards?" I asked Ruben.

"Yeah, sure. I mean, I still work at Berkeley Arts selling art supplies, but I just do that to stay in touch with the common folk," was his reply, which I took to be facetious, especially when both Ivey and Holly raised their eyebrows and smiled.

"Oh, Ruben, you've got a granny ash going," Holly informed Ruben. He looked down at his cigarette, then flicked an inch long ash into the ashtray without a word in reply.

The waiter returned with Sven's drink. As I was paying him, Sven remarked, "It's about time." The waiter ignored him, other than to roll his eyes at me. He picked up my empty beer bottle, then turned to Magdeline and Eva, who both ordered drinks.

"Hey Paulie, does your mother know you're out at this hour?" Holly yelled at a teenaged boy who was loitering on the sidewalk.

"Oh fuck you, Holly," he replied, in a sarcastic tone of voice, "see you back at the house," he added, with a smile.

Holly leaned in close to me and whispered, "He's a local neighborhood kid. 'See you back at the house,' is his stock phrase, he says it to everyone. He's so adorable, he looks like a miniature Mic Jagger."

I looked at Paulie. He was a skinny kid with long, brown hair, a thin face and full lips. *Not a bad looking young man, but who's this Jagger person?* I thought, having heard the name for the second time that evening. Then I leaned in close to Holly, "What's wrong with Ruben's mustache?" I whispered.

She glanced at Ruben, then laughed. "Hey Ruben, your mustache needs a touch-up. Want to borrow my eyebrow pencil?"

"Oh, thanks, got one," he said, pulling an eyebrow pencil from his coat pocket as he stood, then walked toward the men's room.

FAT FREE!

AMERICA

UNITED STATES OF A...

IN GOD WE TRUST

ONE

VOTE

Can Wet Dreams
Cause VD?

"I Dreamed That My
Grandmother Bit me."

Why Not
Save His
Sperm?'

"He draws it on," Holly explained, as Ruben walked away.

Then a man passed our table leading a teenaged girl. "A bar is no place for a young lady, and that's the end of it," I heard him say to her in a stern tone of voice.

"That's Ed and his daughter Ana," Holly whispered to me. "They live nearby. She's so cute, look at that hair do. Oh, and look, now she's putting on her pouty-face," she giggled. "Millie! Oh, Millie," Holly's attention was redirected to an old lady who was dressed like someone from an early 20th century Hollywood movie about the Lower East Side.

"Are you behaving yourself?" the old lady asked Holly in an unusual accent.

Is that a Yiddish accent of some sort? I wondered.

"Always, Millie," Holly replied.

"Want your picture taken?" Millie asked, holding up a Polaroid instant camera. I recognized it as such because I had seen one in a museum in San Francisco. It was part of a traveling exhibition titled, "Rochester NY, the First Silicon Valley."

"No Millie, not tonight. Maybe next week, it's end of the month you know," Holly declined Millie's offer.

Holly's statement made me think, so I asked, "Holly, what is the date today?"

"It's Saturday, the 26th of May," she answered.

"It is the exact same day and date in 2063."

"Really?" she said.

"Yes, it was Saturday, the 26th of May when I woke up this morning," I told her.

"El Futuro, how old are you?" Holly asked.

"Fifty-one," I answered.

"Fifty-one! I would have guessed thirty-one, at most. Gee, I thought Vale looked good for his age. What's your secret?"

"I have no secret. I was born in March, 2012 and now I am fifty-one, or at least I was. With the change in the year I have no idea how old I am." While I was responding to Holly I happen to notice that the beautiful woman I had first admired in the back room was eavesdropping on our conversation.

"El Futuro, what's the biggest medical breakthrough in the

future?" Holly posed a question that required some thought.

"Well, I am not a good person to judge that, but let me think… Well, I have a blind aunt, so I guess that is why the technology that lets blind people see with their ears impresses me."

"See with their ears," Snuky joined the discussion. "How do they do that?"

"Similar to the way bats do. They wear a device that sends out ultrasonic sound waves that bounce off things in the environment, then back to the device, which sends them, via Goldtooth transceiver, to transmitters in the patient's ears. The transmitters translate the ultrasonic sound into audible sound. With training the patient is then able to form an image from the sound waves."

"That's not quite like 'seeing with their ears,'" Snuky pointed out.

"No, I am dating myself. When the technology first became widely available I was a teenager. In those days audible sound was used and the patient's ears picked up the reflected sound waves directly. Currently they use ultrasonic sound waves because they produce a more detailed image, but humans cannot hear in the ultrasonic spectrum, so transmitter-translators are needed. So technically you are right, but it is still mostly like 'seeing with your ears.' And I can tell you from experience, compared with the audible system, the ultrasonic system is nowhere near as annoying to those nearby."

"How well do they see?" Snuky pressed me for details.

"Well enough to navigate the streets safely, walk without a cane and make out furniture in a room. They cannot see in color, they have trouble distinguishing between people's faces, and they cannot read or make out images on the screen of a device... uh, a television. On the other hand, their field of vision is theoretically 360 degrees. Overall, it is a great improvement."

"Really. My sister is blind, but if she has to wait until 2063 she'll be dead first," he said, his initial enthusiasm waning.

"I am sorry, but Holly asked," I said.

"Hello Mike... Captain," Holly said loudly in the direction of the sidewalk. I looked and saw the two men I encountered in the Saloon passing by. The smaller man, who wore a top hat, turned, smiled and held his hand up. The tall, grim fellow just turned and nodded. "That's a couple of the local characters, Mike the Spike and Captain Cool. Captain's nice, but Mike's a bit shady," she explained.

"Yes. I encountered them at the Saloon earlier. The tall one is quite frightening," I gave her my opinion of the pair.

At that moment I heard a low rumble. Then I was startled by a very loud roar. I looked to the source and saw that an outlandish, two-wheeled vehicle had stopped in front of the Savoy Tivoli. The long haired rider made a twisting motion on the handle bar, causing another loud roar that reverberated off the surrounding buildings on the narrow street. People on the patio cheered. Then, with another loud roar, the rider took off into the night.

As he did, a couple of middle aged tourists, who seemed like they were lost, caught my attention. As they passed through the motley crowd on the sidewalk, the male wore a look of concern on his face, the female wore a fake smile of acceptance. *It's sort of like she's whistling past the graveyard*, I thought.

"Want to buy a rose?" A familiar booming voice asked.

I turned to see Bill, who I bought a rose from at Enrico's. He was standing on the sidewalk, giving me an imploring look. "I just bought one from you a couple of hours ago at Enrico's," I reminded him.

"Where is it?" he asked.

"I left it on the bar when I went to chase The White Rabbit. Ruben ended up with it."

Bill looked at Ruben.

"I gave it to Holly," Ruben answered.

"And I got tired of carrying it and I threw it away," Holly beamed.

"Aw Holly, don't tell me that," Bill replied. "Give my life some meaning."

"Okay, maybe I got tired of carrying it and I gave it to the cocktail waitress, Janet Planet," Holly changed her story.

"That's better, at least it didn't go to waste. I like Janet Planet," Bill said.

"And she threw it away," Holly quickly added, then laughed.

An expression of disappointment spread over Bill's face.

"Oh Bill, I'm sorry, but I just got tired of carrying it. Here, let me buy another," Holly said, reaching into her purse and rummaging around for her wallet.

As Holly made her transaction with Bill, I glanced around the room. Nervous movement registered in my peripheral vision. I turned my head to look and saw that the beautiful woman at the table to my left was absentmindedly fanning her legs under her table. *Her legs are so beautiful.* Then I noticed something else; it appeared she wasn't wearing underwear. I looked to reassure myself this wasn't the case, but each time she opened her legs I could see pubic hair. I quickly looked away thinking, *I must have imagined that. She must be wearing black panties.* I couldn't help myself from looking again, just to make sure. When I did she stopped fanning her legs and held them wide open. I had no doubt now. I reflexively looked up and she was looking directly at me, smiling.

I looked away, blushing, then stood, saying to my table mates, "Excuse me, I need to use the restroom," and quickly walked away. My abrupt departure prompted Holly to yell at my back, "Hey, El Futuro, got a prostate problem?"

I didn't really need to use the restroom, but I didn't know where else to go. On my way I passed Ruben, who was returning to the patio, mustache restored. I walked back into the main barroom, walked down the dead end hallway, then entered the men's room. *Since I am here I might as well go*, I thought, as I unzipped my fly at the urinal. *What am I going to do? What was I thinking? It is so humiliating.* I sensed a presence and turned my head slightly. The beautiful woman was standing behind me, looking over my shoulder at my penis. "What are you doing?" I said, quickly putting my penis back into my pants and zipping up.

"I showed you mine, so I get to see yours," she said with a smile.

"I... I have to go," I said, starting for the door, but she grabbed my arm.

"Take me with you, El Futuro. Take me to the future with you. I hate it here. I've always thought I was born too late but meeting you made me realize I was born way too early," she pulled me close, hooked her leg around the back of mine and pulled up her skirt. "Fuck me," she demanded.

"We have not met. I do not even know your name," I said,

pulling free of her grasp and starting for the door. I made it to just outside the men's room when she grabbed my arm again.

"My name is Paula. Come with me." She took me by the hand and pulled me around a corner, through an opening behind the bar, then into a long, dark passage.

"What is this place?" I asked.

"I don't know. I think it used to be a passageway for the guys who delivered the beer. I think it opens onto the sidewalk on Grant, or used to anyways. I know this guy, Eric, he showed it to me." She pushed me against the wall, hooked her leg around mine again, pulled up her skirt and began rubbing her crotch against my thigh. "Fuck me," she whispered seductively into my ear, as she fumbled with the button on the waistband of my pants.

"Please do not do that," I objected, as I felt myself becoming aroused. I pushed her hand away from my waistband and said, "You are very attractive, but I cannot let you engulf me here, in this... alley. Not like this. But you have made me think; I have been so obsessed with getting my device back from The White Rabbit, I never thought about how I am going to return to the future. Or if that is even possible."

"I'm sorry, El Futuro, but I'm desperate," she said, relaxing her hold on me. "I need to get out of here before it's too late. If I can help you get back to the future, will you take me with you?"

"Well, I guess if you can, sure. Why not?" I realized I was in a desperate situation and couldn't be too choosey about help that was being offered. "Oh, I am currently on a date with a woman named Sarah. That might complicate things."

"Look, you take me to the future with you and we'll deal with that when we come to it," Paula said.

"What do you propose?"

"I know this guy, Luther. He's smart. He'll know what to do. Come with me, I'll take you to see him." Paula took my hand and pulled me out of the passageway, then through the barroom past tables and chairs, an old upright scale where a man was weighing himself, and finally a juke box. A couple of more steps and we reached the door which she pushed open and we descended two steps to the sidewalk. Then we turned to our right, she let go of my hand, took me by the arm and we began walking up Grant Avenue.

"Are you really fifty-one?" Paula asked.

"Yes," I answered, noticing that I was forced to walk with a slight limp due to charley horsed calf muscles. At first I was perplexed by this development, but then I remembered vigorously dancing to The Offs, if that was dancing.

As we walked past the patio of the Savoy Tivoli, Holly yelled, "Have fun kids."

Embarrassed I said nothing. I looked at Paula. She was looking straight ahead, smiling. "I hate that bitch," she said.

Luther Blue's
Chapter 9

DJACENT TO THE SAVOY TIVOLI WAS A STORE FRONT WITH A sign that read, Lenny Lerner's Comedy Closet. As we passed it laughter floated out onto the street.

A bit further up the street was a sign that read, Romeo's Dry Goods, with the subtitle, The Working Man's Store. I looked in and saw that the shopkeeper was a little old man with a giant hearing aid who was sitting behind a counter on a raised platform. On shelves behind him men's work pants were stacked high. Standing in front of the counter were two men who were talking with the shopkeeper; one was Captain Cool, the other was Mike the Spike. I stopped to look in while Paula tried pulling me forward, but for some reason I was intrigued.

The shopkeeper was writing something in a small note book. When he finished he spun it around, pushed it across the counter toward Mike the Spike, then handed him the pen. Mike bent forward and also wrote something. The shopkeeper gave him some cash. Mike shoved the cash into his pocket, then stepped back from the counter to reveal The White Rabbit, who had been standing behind the larger man.

My first impulse was to enter and demand that my device be returned, but good sense prevailed. *The two u-bees look dangerous. My biggest problem is that I have to get back to 2063. Forget the device, it can be replaced,* I convinced myself.

"What is it?" Paula asked.

"Oh nothing. I thought I saw something," I lied, and we continued up the street.

Next to Romeo's, on the corner of Grant and Union was an old butcher shop whose sign read, R. Iacopi & Co. It had two windows in the front, a large one to the right side of the door and a small one to the left, with another large window around the corner on the Union Street side.

I stopped here as well, because in the small window to the left of the door was a line of sausages hanging from an iron rack that wrapped around to the Union Street side. The sausages were in various stages of curing, with fresh ones at the front on the Grant Avenue side and fully cured ones around the corner on the Union Street side. The marble shelf below the sausages was lined with butcher paper to catch the fat that dripped from the sausages as they cured in the sun. I deduced that the butcher simply pulled the fully cured sausages off the rack at the end on the Union Street side, slid the still curing ones around toward the end, then hung fresh ones at the beginning on the Grant Avenue side. The simplicity of the sausage curing process fascinated me for a moment. "Okay, we can go," I finally said to Paula, who was tugging on my arm.

We turned from the butcher shop and crossed Grant Avenue. "Let's cross here," Paula said, and we crossed to the other side of Union. "The Italian-French," she said, gesturing to a bakery in an old, yellow brick building on the corner. "If you go to the back door after four in the morning the bakers will sell you a baguette straight out of the oven. This guy I know, Eric, he bought me one once," she told me as we started walking downhill. "This is Malvina's, it's a cafe I go to sometimes," Paula said, as we passed a cafe that shared the building with the Italian-French bakery, then crossed a small, dead end alley. "And this is Cadell Place," she said, gesturing to an ancient wooden building that was painted light blue with white trim. "It's a good breakfast place. It's run by lesbians. If we can't get to the future tonight, we can go there for breakfast in the morning, my treat."

At the bottom of the hill she pointed out Rossi's Pharmacy, which was on the corner of Stockton and Union, across the street from a park that was shrouded in darkness. "Everything around here seems to be owned by a Rossi or a Figoni," Paula mentioned casually, as we crossed Stockton. "Don't walk through this park at night," she cautioned, "I have a friend who was mugged in there last December."

"What is the name of this park?" I asked on a hunch.

"Washington Square Park," Paula answered.

"I thought so, but it looks different than I remember," I said.

"Different, how so?" she asked.

"Well, as I know it, it is well lit, so you can actually see it," I answered, looking at the pitch black void behind the trees that ringed the park. As we proceeded we came to a huge, gnarled tree that was bent over until its trunk almost rested on the ground, then it redirected itself and grew upwards.

Paula pointed out a cafe across the street from the gnarled tree, "That's Mario's. I go there quite a bit. In fact if we can't get to the future tonight, we can have coffee there in the morning... "

"My treat," I cut her off before she finished her sentence. She turned, looked at me and smiled. Then she nudged me to the right at the corner and we began walking up Columbus Avenue. "That's the Pagoda Palace," she pointed out an old movie theater across the street. "It's where the Cockettes used to perform."

Beyond the theater, on the next corner, was a sign on a poll that read, Tony's Service Station. Below that was an area where removable plastic letters and numbers were attached to say, "Carter's Price: Regular $0.92 $^9/_{10}$ Premium $0.96 $^9/_{10}$."

"What does that sign mean?" I asked.

"Oh, that guy Tony who owns the gas station, he's a Republican and he always puts up political sayings or his opinion, whatever. Sometimes it's pretty hilarious, when you think about it. That's where Survival Research Laboratories had their first performance. They did it on a Sunday morning when the station was closed. Tony would be furious if he knew," she explained, though I didn't understand what she was talking about.

We crossed Filbert Street, first to a small traffic island, then to the corner and walked past a restaurant with red and white, checkered table cloths on the tables. It had a sign that read, Tony's Ravioli Factory. Paula saw me reading the sign and said, "Same guy. He owns both corners." Then she asked, "What's the government like in 2063?"

"It is what we call libertarian."

"Oh, we have that. There's this guy, Lyndon LaRouche, I think he's libertarian. He runs in every election for president and he always loses. In fact I just picked up one of his flyers today on Market Street. It's for next year's election. I'll show it to you when we get to my apartment. It'll crack you up, he's a real nut," Paula said.

"I would guess that it is a bit different than that. But I was not born until the second decade of the 21st century and I never studied 20th century history in college. We studied it in my junior year of high school, so I only know the basics about 20th century politics. What I do know is, as soon as the Libertarians gained power they finished the job started by the Reagan Administration and turned almost all government duties over to the corporations."

"Ronald Reagan?" she asked.

"Yes," I replied.

"He becomes president?" she asked, in an incredulous tone.

"Yes, in 1981."

"But he was a terrible governor. He's why there are so many crazy street people in San Francisco, in fact they call them, 'Ronnie's Kids.' And he hates students and poor people," Paula told me.

I was dumbfounded by her statement, it was one of the worst examples of forbidden speech I had ever heard. I was taught in high school that Ronald Reagan was the architect of the modern republic. I reflexively looked around to see if anyone could have heard her comment, then thought, *Damn! My device will have heard that.* I quickly regained my composure when I remembered The White Rabbit had my device and it was the year 1979. I was finally able to reply, "I am sorry, but it is true."

"So corporations run the government in the future?" She asked.

"Yes. But there was a book titled *Convenience* that came out last year... well, many years in your future. It was censored almost immediately, but I was able to read most of the first chapter before it was erased from my device. In it the authors make the claim that ultimately, even the corporations do not run things."

"What does that mean?" she asked.

"Well, the dedication reads, 'To the human body, which is 60 percent water.' It was co-authored by a man and woman who had the same last name, possibly a husband-wife team. Or maybe brother-sister. The gist of their premise is, since water takes the path of least resistance, for the most part, so do humans. 'The path of least resistance' is what we call 'convenience,' and in seeking convenience, people inadvertently dictate the course of history."

"Huh," she said, and I realized I was boring her.

"Where are we going?" I asked, to change the subject and because I wondered where this woman I barely knew was taking me.

"Oh, don't worry, we're almost there," she assured me.

After we passed a dilapidated auto-service station the street became quite dark. At the first store front we came to, Paula let go of my arm and stepped into its recessed entryway. I remained on the sidewalk, nervous about the dark, deserted street. In high school history class we were taught that street violence was rampant in the 20th century. Her earlier comment about a mugging in the park didn't help. *I am carrying a large amount of cash, by current standards. If I lose it I can't get more,* I thought nervously, as I looked around to see if any u-bee ruffians were approaching. I looked at a sign posted above the window that read, Luther Blue. The interior lights of the shop were off. "This place looks closed," I said, as I felt a tingling sensation on the back of my neck.

"Oh it is closed," she said, then tapped on a glass panel in the door that had a curtain blocking the view of the interior.

She waited a moment, then knocked loudly. Finally I heard noise behind the door which opened to reveal an intimidating fellow dressed in black with an intense look about him. His hair was thick and dark brown, it rose in the front, then was combed straight back. Covering his face was a two day growth of black stubble. "Oh, hi Paula. Glad you could make it. Who's your friend?" he spoke with a slight Brooklyn accent.

"Hi Luther. This is El Futuro, he's from the future. He's cool."

"The future?" Luther gave me a once-over, "Nice jacket. I would have guessed Europe. Come in," he said, standing aside as we entered.

He locked the door, then led us through his shop which was filled with extreme looking clothes that hung from chrome plated clothes racks. The clothes were mostly black and featured

gratuitous zippers, studs and grommets. There were also maga-
zines, handmade booklets, colorful badges with clever sayings,
costume jewelry with unusual designs and a jumble of other
things. In a rack displaying postcards, I recognized several of
Ruben's designs. Three guitars hung on the back wall and on a
shelf below them were two black boxes that looked like smaller
versions of the speakers I saw at the Mabuhay. In the corner was
what I recognized as a color Xerox machine, because I saw one
in the same exhibition where I saw the polaroid camera.

At the back of the room Luther stopped in a small hallway,
put his hand on a door knob then said, "They're all downstairs.
Just go on down and help yourself to beer from the ice chest," he
gestured to a doorway opposite the door he was about to enter.
"I'll be down in a minute, I have to use the can." He entered what
I presumed was a restroom and closed the door.

Paula stepped through the opposing doorway, then led the
way down a flight of stairs. We descended through a cloud of
tobacco smoke and entered a basement where tapestries hung on
the walls. Scattered around the room were a number of people
sitting on various pieces of well worn, mismatched furniture. In
the corner, at the front of the room, was a box. In the box was a
spinning, black disk. The box was connected by wires to two
speakers that emitted music at, what was for me, a high volume.
As the disk spun, a stylist glided over its surface, rising and falling
as the obviously warped disk rotated. *A turntable with a vinyl record
and speakers. So primitive and simple, yet it works,* I thought.

Paula took me by the hand and led me to an ice chest that was
on the floor near the turntable. She opened it and pulled two cans
of beer from the ice. "Here," she said, handing me one of the cans.
She used her thumb nail to pry a metal tab upwards on the top of
the can. She put the can to her lips and took a sip. After swallowing
she threw her head back and opened her mouth wide, "Ahhaaa,"
she hissed with satisfaction, then turned and smiled at me.

Then she led me to a small sofa that was covered with an old
blanket. Nearby, the man in a black leather jacket and blue jeans
that I had seen as I re-entered the back room of the Savoy Tivoli,
was leaning against the wall. He was talking with a man who had

dark, reddish hair and was sitting in an old, overstuffed arm chair. I recognized him as a member of The Offs. Sitting on the arm of the chair, with her arm around him was Christine, the beautiful woman in the iridescent, pink raincoat I saw in the back room of the Savoy Tivoli.

As Paula and took seats on the sofa, the man with reddish hair was mid-sentence, "... and yes, we had a great time. They gave us a great reception in New York. We're already planning another trip back east, but San Francisco is our home. It's been good to us and we have no immediate plans to move. I'm serious, Howie."

"'No immediate plans,' but you do plan to move there and leave me in the lurch, after all I've done to help you, Billy," Howie replied.

"Ah, you're paranoid Howie. If a move is in our future it won't be until at least next year," Billy replied.

"What you've done to help us, what about what we've done to help you? And, by-the-way, Howie, a year's a long time in this business," the singer with heavy eye makeup added.

"Don's right, Howie," Christine said, "And I think I'd know if they had any plans to move soon."

"Unless I was planning to ditch you," Billy said to Christine, which prompted her to slap his shoulder, then kiss him on the lips.

"Breeders," Don said, in a disparaging manner, as he watched his friends kiss.

The music stopped and was replaced by a hissing sound that was accompanied by a dull thumping sound. A man rose from where he was sitting on another sofa and walked over to the turn table. He lifted the stylist, then removed the record and slid it into its cardboard sleeve. Then he began looking through an assortment of colorful record sleeves that lay on the floor by the turntable. He was wearing a black T-shirt and I could see that he was heavily tattooed from the wrists up and the neck down.

As I watched him I was distracted by loud knocking on the door upstairs. Then I heard the muffled sound of a man yelling, but he was too far away for me to make out what he was saying. Then I heard a toilet flush, followed by the sound of the front door being opened. A man's voice said something to which I heard

Luther respond, "I heard you, but I was taking a shit." Soon
Luther and a man I didn't know descended the stairway. The new-
comer was laughing as they reached the basement. "Oh, fuck you,
Eric," Luther said with a grin, as they seated themselves on folding
chairs against the front wall of the basement.

As soon as Eric was seated, he began greeting those in the
room, "Don Off, Billy Off, and Bob Off... What you guys need is
a band member named Jack." He laughed at his own joke then
continued, "Hey, Howie. And Christine, how are you?" Both
Howie and Christine nodded in response. "Steeler, Jimmy, Penelope, Reesa," he greeted four people who were sitting in the back of
the room. They sat facing each other; the two women sat with their
backs to the room, the two men with their backs to the wall. "Oh,
hey Luther, I forgot to tell you," Eric changed the subject, "I went
to a party up at the Wicket mansion in Pacific Heights last week."

"Really? I've heard stories about it, but I've never been.
What's it like?" Luther asked.

"Oh Luther, you'd go crazy over this place. To start with,
Laffing Sal from Playland at the Beach is in the entryway, there's
a tiger skin rug on the floor below her, and that's just the start.
Old man Wicket must have a thousand chess sets and they're set
up all over the ground floor on tables, chairs, whatever. Upstairs
he has bedrooms where he lets people crash and the hallway up
there has about a hundred black monkey pelts nailed to the wall.
And instead of doors, the bedrooms just have sheer, black material hung in them—the place is *tres* gothic. I mean, I can't even
begin to describe all that I saw."

"I've heard of that place. I know someone who stayed there
for two months, rent free," the heavily tattooed man turned from
looking through the record sleeves to comment on Eric's story.

"Bob, the place is indescribable," Eric replied, then he looked
at Paula. "Oh hi, Paula. I didn't see you sitting there."

Without looking at Eric, Paula shrugged and said nothing.

"You're not still mad about the other night, are you?" Eric
said, then laughed in a carefree manner.

Paula squirmed in her seat and shrugged again.

Looking at Eric I judged him to be very handsome, almost

as handsome as he seemed to think he was. He was also very charming, in an annoying sort of way.

Paula turned to me, "Maybe we should go," she said quietly.

"But I thought you said Luther knew a way for me, I mean us, to get back to 2063," I quietly replied.

Eric stood, then stepped up to us. "Sorry man, my name's Eric, what's yours?" he held out his hand.

A hissing sound filled the room briefly, then the music began, ... *You can get it if you really want...*

"This is the greatest album of all time," tattooed Bob said, before returning to his seat.

For the first time Paula looked at Eric. "His name is El Futuro," she said, in an annoyed tone of voice.

"Yes, that's what some people call me," I said, standing to shake Eric's hand. As I did, Paula grabbed my left hand. When our handshake ended, Paula pulled me back down beside her with a jerk on my hand, then draped her arm over my shoulders.

"Paula, you know you mean a lot to me. More than you know," Eric said, bending down to look her in the eyes.

"Really?" Paula said, in a confrontational tone of voice.

"Of course, what do you think?" Eric stood upright. "You don't think that Jane means anything to me, do you?" He stopped to laugh for emphasis. "I know her boyfriend, Larry. Larry's a friend of mine."

"Well it seemed like she meant something to you Thursday night. You left me standing at the Deaf Club wondering where you went. I felt like such a fool!"

"Paula, that was just business. Jane had something I wanted and I knew that I had to act fast. As soon as I got it I came right back to the Deaf Club, looking for you."

"Really?" Paula said, her tone softening as she slowly slid her arm off of my shoulders.

"Yes, really," Eric answered, his face adopting an overly serious expression.

I didn't know Eric at all, but it was obvious to me that he was lying. I barely knew Paula, but it was obvious to me that she wanted to believe him.

"Paula, I have something I want to show you. Come with

me for a minute." Eric looked at me, "El Futuro, will you excuse us for a moment?" he asked.

"Sure," I said, knowing I had already lost.

Paula stood, "I'll be right back," she said emphatically, and they both walked up the stairs.

"*Ciao*," Eric said over his shoulder to the room.

"Better lock the door," Luther said, standing and starting for the stairs.

There was a commotion upstairs as the door was opened. I heard what sounded like a glass bottle breaking on pavement. Next I heard Eric say, "Where'd you guys come from?" A man's voice answered, though I couldn't make out what he said. Then several people laughed. "Funny man," was the last thing I heard Eric say before I heard the door being closed and then locked again.

Luther must have heard what I heard, because he stopped climbing the stairs, turned and came back into the basement.

Soon a procession appeared at the top of the stairs, led by Ruben Dann. Ruben stood motionless for a moment, then dove chest first down the stairs. He slid on his chest, almost to the bottom, then came to a stop, stood and held his arms in the air triumphantly.

Riotous laughter erupted from the head of the stairs. A woman loudly declared, "Paaarty central!" I looked up and saw Ivey with a lit cigarette dangling from her lips. She carried a brown, paper sack in one hand, a bottle of wine in the other and clutched her stack of calendars under her arm. As she descended the stairway she was followed by Holly and a well dressed couple that I didn't recognize. I held feint hope that Paula would be with them, but Sven was the last in line.

"Hey Ruben, here's your beer," Ivey said, holding out the brown, paper sack to a disoriented Ruben.

Ruben took the sack as the other members of his entourage descended the stairway.

"That was quite an entrance, Ruben," Tattooed Bob commented from where he sat.

"Thanks Bob," an obviously inebriated Ruben replied, pulling a bottle of Miller High Life from his sack.

"Lenny," Luther said, as he shook the hand of the man I

didn't know, who was bald and wore a silver gray suit with a white shirt and a skinny, pink tie. At his side stood a lovely brunette dressed in red and black. "Teresa," Luther said, as he shook her hand. "Sven, Holly, Ivey, Ruben," he completed his greetings, nodding at each person as he said their name. "Take a seat where you can find one. Beer's in the ice chest. Did you guys lock the door?" Luther asked those newly arrived, making sure his fortress was secure.

"Yes, Luther, I did," Sven said.

Lenny and Teresa sat on two folding chairs against the front wall, Sven took a seat on a sofa next to tattooed Bob. Ivey and Ruben remained standing and Holly came over to the sofa where I sat. "This seat taken?" she asked, her bare legs momentarily filling my field of vision.

"No," I replied, quickly reminding myself to look up before my gaze lingered too long on her legs.

Holly sat next to me, then said, "I saw Paula leaving with Eric. She's a very pretty girl, but that Eric is quite the ladies man."

I could tell she was trying to console me, and though part of me was disappointed, mostly I was relieved. I had realized, back when Paula was knocking on Luther's door, that she was more than I could handle.

"So Lenny, is Sh-Boom going to take out an ad in *Nart*?" Ivey asked.

"No, Ivey, I'm sorry," Lenny answered. I noticed that he spoke with an English accent. "Our advertising budget is either used up or already allocated for this year. Any extra money is going into our Ace & The Eights recording project."

"When is *Nart* coming out?" Tattooed Bob asked.

"Mid summer is what we're shooting for," Ivey answered.

"Ah, that means late summer," tattooed Bob said with a smile.

"I think we'll make mid summer," Ruben disagreed.

"Let's see, it's all punk rock artists working on a magazine together. Make that fall," tattooed Bob adjusted his estimate.

"Hey Ruben, speaking of *Nart*, have you come up with something for your graphic page yet?" Ivey asked.

"Yeah, I got a paste-up that's half finished. It's got two Egyptian gods sitting in the background, facing each other. One of them is holding a donkey, the other an elephant. I got Tut's face in the foreground and a row of businessmen holding briefcases along the bottom under Tut's face. That's all I got so far, but I already know what the caption is: Tut's Dead."

"Wha, wha... haaa!" Ivey responded loudly. "You can't say that," she said. Then she coughed, took a drag on her cigarette, a gulp of wine, then laughed again.

"Tut?" I looked at Holly for an explanation.

"King Tut," she replied. Then she explained, "There's an exhibition at the De Young that's opening next month of stuff from King Tut's tomb. It's a big deal."

There was commotion in the back of the room. When I redirected my attention I saw that the four people, who had been sitting in the back talking, were now leaving. "Hey Luther, thanks a lot, man. We're going to the Target Video party, it starts in about an hour and we want to stop at the Grub Stake for burgers on the way. If anybody needs a ride my van's parked right outside," a tall imposing fellow with a shaved head offered conveyance to those present.

"Thanks, Steeler, but I'm getting a ride with Lenny and Teresa," Holly said.

"Howie is giving me, Billy and Christine a ride, we'll meet you there," Don said.

"I'm going to stay Steeler, I'm starting a new tattoo on a regular customer tomorrow," tattooed Bob said.

"I can't make it either, I have to help Ruby develop the film she's shooting tonight," Ivey said.

"I'll go," Ruben accepted the offer. "My 30th birthday is Tuesday and I'm spreading out the celebration," he slurred.

Sven also joined those leaving and Luther walked upstairs to let them out.

"Who were those two women with Steeler?" I asked Holly.

"The blond with short hair is Penelope, she's the singer for the Avengers. The brunette with long hair is Ressa, Jimmy's girlfriend. Jimmy was the other guy, he's the guitar player for the Avengers." she told me.

"Oh," I replied, thinking there were an unusual number of attractive women in this crowd.

I heard the door being opened, some people talking, then the door was closed and locked again.

"I decided to stay," Ruben announced, as he descended the stairs, this time in a normal fashion. He was followed by a petite blond and she was followed by two members of the Mutants that I recognized from the show at the Mabuhay.

"Beer's in the ice chest," Luther said, from the back of the line on the stairs. "Help yourself."

"Hi, De De," Holly said to the petite blond, as she stood to greet her.

Ruben and the two Mutants stopped at the bottom of the stairs and began a conversation. Ruben handed each of the Mutants a bottle of beer from his paper sack, then went to the ice chest to put the remaining two beers from his sack into the ice. Then he returned to where the Mutants stood, and Ivey walked over to join their conversation.

"Where's Sallier and Sue?" Ivey asked the two Mutants.

"They're at Target Video, they're doing a performance tonight. We're driving over there after this if you want a ride. I got my truck, so you'd have to squeeze in between me and Dave, unless you want to ride in the bed," the tall, blond guitar player said.

"Oh thanks, John, but I got to go home soon to feed Rattler and help Ruby develop film," Ivey declined John's offer of a ride.

"Scooch over," Holly said to me, as she and De De sat next to me on the small sofa. "El Futuro, this is De De, she's the singer for UXA. De De, this is El Futuro, he's from the future," she introduced me. Then she and De De began a conversation.

While Holly was talking with De De, and Ivey and Ruben were talking with the two Mutants, I was left alone with my thoughts. I had to admit that it was looking increasingly unlikely that I would be able to find a way to return to the future. *But this morning it would have looked even more unlikely that I would find myself in 1979 by nightfall*, I reasoned, in my unreasonable situation. *If I can't get back to the future, I have to find a place to sleep for the night.*

When a break came in Holly and De De's conversation, I interrupted them. "Holly, if I cannot find a way back to the future, would I be able to stay at your place tonight?" I realized how that sounded, but not until after it left my lips.

"Aw, El Futuro, I would but my place is really tiny and I don't think my boyfriend would like it," Holly answered.

"I am sorry, I know how that sounded, but I am desperate," I responded. Then I changed the subject, hoping to put the uncomfortable feeling my comment left in the air behind me, "I did not know you had a boyfriend. Where is he?"

"Oh, Bobby's not into punk. He never goes to shows. He's a comedian and tonight he's out at the Holy City Zoo on Clement to see some new comic. He said Robin Williams will be in the audience. He says Robin Williams is to comedy what the Ramones are to punk. Bobby's a real crack-up, he's a fast talking New Yorker," she outlined her relationship for me, then returned to her conversation with De De.

I noticed that Luther was not engaged in a conversation, so I excused myself from Holly and De De and went to where he stood looking through the record sleeves. "Excuse me, Luther," I said.

He looked up from the record sleeve he held in his hand. "Yeah, El Futuro, what's up?"

"Well, I know this may sound very strange, but Paula said you might know a way for me to return to the year 2063, which is where I come from and where I belong."

"You're right pal, that is very strange," Luther replied. "Look, I don't know what Paula was talking about. I wish I could help you, but I can't," he said, then went back to reading the record sleeve.

I should have known better, I thought, as I returned to the sofa.

I sat next to Holly and when a break came in her conversation with De De I told her, "I asked Luther and he cannot help me. I am beginning to worry about my situation."

"I'm sorry, El Futuro, I wish I could help but I don't know anything about time travel," she said sympathetically. "Maybe you could get a hotel room for the night. There are some cheap ones around North Beach. I've heard that the Saint Paul is a good one."

"Or, you could just drop this whole 'El Futuro' business," De De addressed me for the first time since our introduction. "Nobody buys it, I know I don't. They're just humoring you." I was shocked that this petite blond with a pixie hairdo and angelic face was speaking to me like some sort of u-bee. "You think you can just barge into this crowd, get people to pay attention to you and get laid. I heard you proposition Holly," is how she finished her thoughts on the subject of me.

"Oh, De De, leave him alone. He's harmless," Holly came to my defense.

"Ah... " I struggled for a response. "De De, I know how that sounded, but I really am worried about where I am going to stay tonight. I did not stop to think about the nuance of my words."

"Well, while we're on the subject of 'your words,' you might want to think about using a contraction or two. As it is it takes you twice as long as it should to say anything," she critiqued my speech.

"Look, De De, I do not want to... "

"*Don't* want to, damn it! *Don't*," she corrected me.

"I do... I dooon't want to make trouble," I forced myself to use a contraction.

"See, was that so hard?" She asked.

"No. But it did feel strange and unnatural," I said as I stood. "I think I should leave, I need to get a hotel room before it is too late."

"Do-not-do-me-an-y-fav-ors," De De said, slowly and sarcastically, altering her voice to sound robotic.

"Oh, El Futuro, it's just a misunderstanding. Don't go," Holly said.

"I think it would be for the best. I have to find some kind of way out of here," I replied, starting for the stairs.

Ivey was standing by the stairs, talking with Ruben and the two Mutants. As I approached she was mid sentence, "... ah, the curse of the easily amused," she finished her sentence, then laughed.

Then she redirected her attention to me, "So, El Futuro, how goes it? Leaving already? Guys, this is El Futuro," she introduced me. "El Futuro, this is John Mutant and Dave Mutant."

"Pleased to meet you," I said, to the two Mutants that I recognized as the drummer and the guitar player, but was too distracted to be more cordial. "Ivey, I do not blame you if you do not believe I am from the future, but I am and I need to get back there. I do not belong here," I said.

"Huh. Well, there's really nothing I can do to help... Well you know, I have this neighbor, Michael. He's a bit eccentric, but if anybody can help you it would be him. I should go home soon anyway, I have to feed my cat, Rattler. And I'm helping Ruby develop the film she's shooting tonight. Michael lives in our building. Come with me," she said, then led me up the stairs. "Night Luther, thanks a lot, got to go," she yelled over the music.

"Good night, El Futuro. Good luck getting home," Holly yelled to me.

"Thanks, Holly," I answered loudly, as I followed Ivey up the stairs with Luther following close behind.

Michael's
Chapter 10

A S WE EXITED LUTHER BLUE'S I HEARD LUTHER LOCK THE door behind us. We turned to our right, then began walking up Columbus Avenue.

Two doors from Luther Blue's we walked past a store that was closed. The lights were off and the interior was dark, but hanging in the window, glowing brightly, was a red neon sign that read, Postcard Palace. "This must be one of the places Ruben said he sells his postcards," I commented.

"Oh, yeah. I know Barbara and Diane who run the place. They have great art openings there," Ivey said, as we left the postcard shop behind.

Ivey was in a talkative mood and I was feeling the effects of more alcohol than I was used to, so I let her do the talking. She told me that she and Ruby moved to San Francisco together from Buffalo, New York. I congratulated myself for guessing that Ruby's accent was from upstate New York. The rest of Ivey's conversation consisted primarily of antidotes about the local punk scene and details of a trip she and Ruby once took to Egypt. I feigned attention to her stories, but mostly I concerned myself with staying aware of my surroundings.

At the end of the block we passed a store on the corner that had garish wigs displayed in the window. Then we crossed a side street where a row of cars were parked perpendicular to the curb. Sitting unused in the dark, these cars seemed a waste of such expensive pieces of equipment. Then I noticed a scruffy individual lurking between two of the cars. He appeared to be in the process of breaking into one of them. This worried me, as he kept a wary eye on us as we passed through his domain.

However Ivey, who I'm sure saw him, seemed unconcerned with him or his activities and continued with her stories.

Next we passed a playground that was next to the North Beach Library, and then a triangular plot of asphalt filled with parked cars. At one corner of the triangular plot a large sign proclaimed it to be a parking lot. I was impressed by the sign that was painted freehand, with lots of color and embellishments. The parking lot was encircled by steel posts with a chain strung between them, presumably to prevent unauthorized parking.

Further up the street we came to an odd looking building that seemed out of place. It was several stories tall and was built from unadorned cast concrete on a narrow plot of land that was adjacent to a vacant lot, all of which made it look unusually thin. Near the top Bekins Storage was painted in a bold typeface with clunky, square serifs. As we passed it I noticed that someone had written on its wall, "One world, one building."

Finally we came to a stretch of Columbus Avenue where three streets crossed one another, forming a large intersection. We crossed Chestnut Street, then Taylor Street, where the cable car cable whirled beneath the cable car tracks. Once we crossed Taylor, we started to cross Columbus, but had to wait for the pedestrian light. Near where we were standing was a triangular bar. Two of its patrons came out of a door on the point of the triangle and began cursing at one another. Suddenly one of them punched the other and a fight broke out. Several additional patrons came out onto the sidewalk, some to break up the fight, others just to watch. Luckily the light changed and I was happy to put some distance between myself and the crowd of drunken u-bee ruffians.

As we were crossing the street, I looked up in time to see a car run the red light. I held my arm out to stop Ivey, who was busy talking and didn't take notice. The car whizzed by a scant three feet from us. As it passed us I saw the driver in silhouette with a bottle in his mouth, his head tipped back.

"Fuck you, asshole!" Ivey yelled at him, and we continued to the other side.

People driving cars is insanity, I thought, shaking from an adrenalin rush. We stepped onto the curb, turned to our right and walked past an old, impressive entertainment venue that took up the entire block. It's facade was well lit and it had a large marquee which read, Bimbo's 365. Patrons were spilling out of the club, causing us to negotiate a crowded sidewalk. At the curb, men in white smocks scurried around at a frantic pace. I noticed their smocks had The Flying Dutchman embroidered in red on the back, like the car attendants I saw on Broadway. They pulled cars up to the curb, got out and handed keys to what I assumed were the owners. Then they ran off as soon as they were paid, presumably to get another car. *It does not get much more inconvenient than that*, I thought.

Just past Bimbo's 365 we turned to our left and walked up a frighteningly dark and isolated alleyway named Houston. At the end of Houston we encountered a steep, cement stairway. We climbed the stairs to the top, then turned to our right and began walking downhill on Jones Street. "That's where I live with Ruby and Vale and Annex," Ivey said as we passed a recessed doorway in a large wooden building.

At the corner of Jones and Francisco Streets we climbed a stairway that brought us to a porch which was illuminated by an overhead light. On the porch there were three doors. Ivey knocked on one of them, then she rang the door bell.

As we waited I heard someone descending a stairway. Soon the door was opened by a tall, thin man wearing a blond wig that was slightly askew and a tight fitting, ultramarine blue satin dress with horizontal, chartreuse stripes. "Hello neighbor, have you come to borrow a cup of sugar?" he asked, in a drowsy voice.

"No, Michael, I have this friend with a problem," she said, gesturing to me. "This is El Futuro. El Futuro, this is Michael," Ivey introduced us.

"Yes, well come in," Michael said, then stood aside as we entered. He followed us as we climbed one flight of stairs. At the top of the stairs we entered a living room dominated by a large, round, off-white ottoman, that was set into a bay window. In front of the ottoman, on a small table, was a glass water pipe. The smell of marijuana hung in the air.

In one corner of the room a couple were seated on chairs across a table from one another. The male was bending over the table with his back to us. I heard him inhale vigorously, then he sat up and handed a straw to the woman; it was Eric and Paula.

Eric turned to look at us, while Paula sat holding the straw in her hand, looking at me with an expression of surprise on her face. "Well, this is awkward," Eric said, then laughed uncomfortably.

"I'm sorry, El Futuro," Paula said, "But Eric and I have... well we've been... "

"Do not worry, Paula. I am here for another reason." I turned to our host, "Michael, this may sound strange, but when I woke up this morning it was in the year 2063. How I ended up here in 1979, I do not know, but I am desperate to get back to 2063. Ivey said you might be able to help me."

I heard Paula inhale sharply, then both she and Eric stood. "We got to be going, Michael," Eric said. "Thanks for everything."

"Yes, everything," Paula said, then they quickly slipped out the door.

"I got to go too, Michael. I have to feed Rattler and then I have to set up the darkroom before Ruby gets home," Ivey explained, then she left as well.

After locking the door behind them, Michael hiked up his dress, then sat crosslegged on the ottoman. "Please, sit down," he said, gesturing to a chair across the table from the ottoman. I sat as Michael held a lighter over the bowl of the water pipe and put the mouth piece between his lips. He puffed a few times, inhaled deeply, then removed the mouth piece from his lips and offered it to me. Smoke rose from the bowl of the water pipe.

"No thanks, Michael. Marijuana does not agree with me," I replied.

He shrugged, exhaled and took another drag on the pipe. Finally he stopped and looked at me. "So you're from the future," he said in a strained voice, as he struggled to both speak and hold the smoke in his lungs.

"Yes, I know it is hard to believe, but I swear that it is true," I began to launch into my explanation, but he held up a hand to silence me as he exhaled.

"I didn't say I didn't believe you. I can see and hear that you are from the future. You may find it hard to believe that I am from the year 2096. Or at least I was. Now I quite contentedly live in the year 1979. I arrived here in 1973," Michael explained. "My question for you is: Why do you want to return?"

"Well, that is where I belong, for one thing. I have a good job, a convenient pod, and I have a woman friend. In fact I was on a date with her in an old u-bee bar called The Rabbit Hole when this happened to me," I told him.

"You can get another job. You will meet another woman. So I ask again: Why do you want to return?"

"Because I am not comfortable here. Everything is sort of the same, yet so different, so primitive, so... so inconvenient."

"Inconvenient," Michael said thoughtfully, then took another puff on his pipe. "Have you noticed the way women dress in these times?" he asked.

"Yes, that is part of it. I feel I am in a constant state of arousal. I am not used to that. And everyone I have met acts like a u-bee."

"Ah yes, the u-bees. What percentile were you in, if I may ask?" he said.

"I am a thirty-percenter," I proudly replied.

"I'm afraid that's not much of a buffer. And even in your day it was eroding fairly quickly. By the late 21st century, if you're not in the top twenty percent, you're probably a u-bee yourself, or at least a menial. What is your job?" he asked.

"I am an interior designer," I answered apprehensively. "And technically I am in the top twenty-eight percent," I added.

"Uh-huh, I believe interior designers were u-beed sometime in the 2070s."

"So I only have... "

"About ten years or so," he finished my sentence.

"What percentile were you in?" I asked him, feeling that I should go on the offensive.

"Twelve percent," he answered.

"Twelve percent! That would make you a Controller or a Seer or, or something." I was humbled, never having met someone from that social class.

"Yes, I was a Seer."

"And you do not want to return?" I asked.

"No, I'm happy here. Are you aware of the levels of mental illness that obtain in the future? By 2096 two out of five people in the top income levels will be psychologically realigned in their life time. Some more than once. It wasn't much better in your day."

"I did not know that, but I am willing to take that chance. I cannot stay here."

"El... What is your name? Your real name," Michael asked.

"John, John Simon," I answered.

"You know John, a good rule of thumb is 'Never question the knowledge of a Seer.' But here, let me show you something," he said, as he rose from the ottoman, then crossed the room to an old chest of drawers. He pulled an envelope from the top drawer, then returned to the ottoman and resumed his seat. He pulled a sheet of paper from the envelope and handed it to me. "Read this," he instructed.

I unfolded it and found it was a short note, handwritten in block letters: "Michael, I am leaving you. It is not because of anything you have done. And it is not because of anything I have done. It is because of what they have done to us. Do not try to follow me, you will not find me. All of my love, Estelle."

I handed it back to him when I was finished reading.

Michael picked up a tea cup that was on the window sill next to his ottoman. He took a sip from it, then replaced it on the window sill. Then he put the letter back into the envelope and tossed it next to his tea cup. "The very act of writing that on paper put us both in jeopardy, but it was the only way she had to assure that it wouldn't be read by a surveillance bot as she wrote it. It bought her time. She is, or was, a Seer, and she felt the need to abandon her life.

"When I found that note I went out to find her, but soon realized I never would. If she wanted to disappear, she knew how to do it. She was gone and my life had changed. I was passing an old bar on Columbus and decided to stop and have a drink to calm down. Soon after I bought a drink I needed to use the restroom. Afterwards, as I was returning to the barroom, I noticed drapes at the end of the hallway. My curiosity got the better of me, I went through them and found myself in the year 1973."

"That is exactly what happened to me," I said, noticing that by the way Michael was sitting I could see he was wearing red, bikini briefs under his dress.

"Uh-huh. Well, for the first few days I was as terrified as I assume you are now. I had no money, not any that I could spend anyway, and I was forced to join those who sleep in the park or in doorways. Then a few days turned into a few weeks, I was offered work and I took it."

He stopped talking for a moment, reached into his tea cup and pulled out a mushroom, which he proceeded to eat. Then he resumed his story, "Soon I was living in an SRO and after about a year I rented this place. It turns out that the knowledge I brought with me from the late 21st century gives me certain advantages here in the 1970s. Of course much of it isn't directly applicable, or even mentionable, but I am doing quite well by current standards."

"I do not know if I can last that long, although I am considering getting a hotel room for the night, if you cannot help me, that is," I said.

"John, are you familiar with the old saying, 'Progress has a mind of its own'?"

"'You cannot stop progress,' or something like that. Yes, I am familiar with it."

"That phrase implies that we have no control over progress. How about the phrase, 'the path of least resistance'?"

"Yes, I have heard people use it," I answered.

"While we were in college, Estelle and I co-authored a book based on the combination of those two concepts. It was titled *Convenience.*"

"I read that! Or at least I read most of the first chapter," I told him.

"Yes, the bots censored it almost immediately. I'm glad to hear that someone read some of it. We really took a chance with that. Luckily, both being candidates for Seer at the time, we knew what we were doing. We were able to cover our tracks in a number of ways. We wrote it as if we were a married couple, even though we weren't married at the time and, of course, we changed our names. We did a few other technical things, such as write it on an encrypted computer that Estelle modified so that it was not detectable by the XG Network. Computers like that are called *free boxes,* they are very illegal. We disposed of it as soon as *Convenience* was published.

"Oh, and by the way, just by reading it you sent up a red flag, 'the little bot in the cloud is watching you,'" he cautioned me with an old saying."

Then he continued, "As candidates for Seer, our studies in lower division were fairly general, with an emphasis on history, philosophy, and psychiatry. We wrote *Convenience* in our sophomore year. The idea came from a drunken conversation we had with college friends at the end of our freshman year, about whether humanity could and, if so, would address the problems we all agreed were looming.

"After *Convenience* was published and summarily censored, Estelle and I continued our studies. In upper division our thinking on the subject matter of *Convenience* became more sophisticated. However, the basic premise of our work didn't change, which is that humans are hurtling headlong into a future over which we have no control, anymore than a snail or a fish or a dog does. The difference is, in our case, it's a future largely of our own unwitting creation."

"That is not entirely fair… " I started to come to the defense of humanity, but then remembered I was talking with a Seer, so I bit my tongue.

He gave me a moment to finish my thought, but when an uncomfortable silence began to grow he continued, "I mean, it's not like we didn't have ample notice. We were aware of the problems by the 1970s, we even began to do something about them. For instance, in the year we find ourselves, programs are in place that would have alleviated the environmental catastrophe now unfolding in the 21st century. But in the 1980s we stopped and did a 180 degree turn. That's not a sign of great intelligence. We're clever, curious and industrious, but we usually allow greed to trump intelligence.

"From where I once lived, on the cusp of the 22nd century, the future of humanity looked bleak. For one thing, sea levels were rising. I'm sure you've noticed how San Francisco is shrinking. I believe Ocean Beach was already becoming heavily eroded by the 2030s."

"Yes, I remember that," I answered, thinking of a trip I took to Ocean Beach with college friends when I was in my early twenties.

"It and The Embarcadero were often flooded at high tide by the 2040s, weren't they?"

"Yes, but... "

"Well, those things and more are inundated in the 2090s." With that he abruptly changed the subject, "In the early 2080s I heard a rumor that A.I. finally achieved singularity. It was around that time, probably coincidently, though perhaps not, that the human population stagnated, then began to fall. Once the population began its decline it developed a momentum of its own. Predictions are that by the end of the 22nd century the earth will be down to six billion individuals, with no end in sight. Of course, simple extrapolation isn't a reliable way to predict the future, but one way or another, we were long overdue for a hedge trimming. Humanity had reached infestation levels in the biosphere by the late 20th century, and nature doesn't tolerate infestation for long. But even if the predicted fall in population pans out, it won't be enough to save us from the catastrophe that awaits.

"You know, John, making a distinction between the natural world and the man-made world is a mistake. Have you ever seen San Francisco from the Bay Bridge on your way into The City?"

"Of course I have, ever since I was a little boy," I replied absentmindedly, still trying to digest his previous statements.

"Have you noticed, especially at night in the fog, how The City looks like a natural phenomenon, almost like a coral reef rising out of the bay?"

"I have not thought about it in that way... " I paused to linger on the image he planted in my mind's eye.

"From my view point The City is a natural phenomenon. Have you ever seen a video or read a description of a termite mound and its internal workings? Or of a bee hive?" he asked.

"Yes, I have."

"If those are considered natural phenomenon, why not a city?

And if you take that view, then you're not far from recognizing that the robots are as much a natural phenomenon as we are, they evolved from our minds after all."

"Well, I do not think I can agree with that," I objected, concerned that his rambling discourse was an indication the drugs were getting to him or that maybe he was one of those two out of five people he spoke of.

He ignored me and continued, "Estelle and I always meant to do a follow-up to *Convenience*, to add nuance from what we learned since our first publication and to try to get a larger audience by making our publication undetectable by the bots. Estelle thought she might know a way to do that. We started on the second edition in our senior year of college. But after college we got our positions as Seers, we got married, one thing led to another, and we never finished it. I guess we just gave up, as idealists often do once they find a stable station in life. Do you see those?" He asked, indicating two poster sized graphics on the wall.

"Yes," I answered. Each of the graphics was comprised of a jumble of many small arrows of varying sizes that criss-crossed one large arrow. History was printed at the top of one of the graphics, Grand Conspiracy Theories at the top of the other.

"The one on the left titled *History* is an approximation of an illustration Estelle designed for our second book, the one we never finished. I made that one from memory. It took me two weeks to do both of those graphics, I had to use press type and drafting tape," Michael explained.

"What?" I had no idea what he was talking about.

"That's what I said. But there are no personal computers in the 1970s, so I had to make do with what was available. I had to make them by hand."

"Oh," I replied, still confused, but for the sake of the conversation I left it at that.

"Look at the graphic titled *History*. It and the original were done for illustration purposes, both are a simplification of reality. And since Estelle rendered the original in 3D, I had to further simplify that one because I had to render it in 2D.

"The small arrows represent individuals or organizations that comprise a political body, such as a city or a country. Their varying size represents the varying magnitudes of wealth and power each possess; the larger the arrow, the more wealth and power. The direction they are moving represents what each is striving for. Their relative position represents their political inclination. Those small arrows are known as *vectors*. If you could account for each and every vector, including all of their values, the graphic would be a haze of arrows, most so small they couldn't be seen at this resolution.

"If you average the values for all of those small arrows, you end up with that big arrow, which is the mean vector. In this context, the mean vector represents the course of history, which is the average of all human activity. By tinkering with laws, social conventions, taxes, et cetera, and by appealing to people's sense of convenience, it would seem that you can nudge the arrow of history in the direction you want it to go. That's exactly what the corporations have been trying to do since they rose to dominance in the early 21st century.

"Now, you can't account for each individual entity or know all of their values exactly, but you don't need to. If you take Big Data, which has been collected since the dawn of the 21st century, add to it the knowledge of how to manipulate people's desires, gleaned from over one hundred years of modern advertising, then parse all of that data with the XG Network, you have a powerful tool.

"The second graphic, the one on the right, illustrates one of the flaws in grand conspiracy theories. That one was my idea, it came to me while I was stoned one night. Grand conspiracy theories tend to be very neat and clean: That happened, then this happened, which led to that happening, all neatly aligned and, seemingly, quite plausible. And that's what a grand conspiracy theory is, a straight line of cause and effect. The graphic on the left, depicting the arrow of history, is anything but neat and clean because it represents how life really is: Messy, chaotic and, at times, quite implausible.

"In the graphic on the right the chaotic mess is grayed out and what we're left with is where the vectors cross the mean vector. Look at where the first vector crosses the mean vector at the bottom. If you look at that crossing point, then look up to the next crossing point and the next, you proceed in a straight line along the shaft of

GRAND CONSPIRACY
THEORIES

the mean vector. It's tempting to take the view that you've uncovered a grand conspiracy, where several entities are working in unison for a desired outcome.

"Of course to take that view you have to ignore the fact that, in reality, the arrows are moving in different directions and at cross purposes to one another. But when you narrow your view point to only where the vectors cross the mean vector, and disregard vectors that don't suit your argument, you can make the case that one leads to the next, in a straight line.

"It's primarily the u-bees and menials that are attracted to this type of simplistic, linear thinking. Seers are taught that grand conspiracy theories are the 'pastime of the powerless.' However, I will say this for them, grand conspiracy theories often make more interesting stories than the truth. And that's what they are, story telling among the lower classes. They suspect that they're being duped by the five percent, which they are, but repeating grand conspiracy theories to one another makes them feel that they know what the five percent are up to. They'd be shocked to learn that most of the grand conspiracy theories they are repeating are concocted by members of the fifteen percent working at the behest of the five percent, expressly to manipulate the sixty percent," he ended with a sinister smile.

"But, Michael, it seems to me that you have contradicted yourself," I dared to question the knowledge of a Seer.

"How so?" he asked.

"Well, first you said that humans have no control over progress and where that is leading us, then you said that the corporations are controlling the direction of human progress. Corporations are made up of humans, are they not?"

"Of course they are, but I said they were trying. Look at the graphic depicting history again. All of those little arrows represent entities working at cross purposes to one another because each is, or is comprised of, greedy human beings.

"They aren't working in unison, but their combined momentum did nudge the arrow of history, though not in the exact direction any of them wanted. However, if you were so inclined, you could take the view that since they did manage to nudge the arrow of history, that they conspired to do so.

"But there is no need for a grand plan or a grand conspiracy, nor is there one. It works as it always has since the dawn of time, organically, like natural selection. So even though there are entities doing their best to change the course of history to their own advantage, and having some small and temporary successes here and there, at some point the ability of the corporations, or any entity comprised of human beings, to control the course of history runs up against an immutable object; aggregate human nature. And aggregate human nature is no more controllable or predictable than the weather. So, to reiterate, we are hurtling headlong into the future.

"If that weren't enough, at the dawn of the industrial revolution humanity painted itself into a corner with the constant growth model; in the long run that doesn't work, everyone can see that.

"Our dilemma is, if we don't change course the world will end with a whimper. And as I said, in 2096 that is essentially what is predicted. However, since the modern world is so intertwined, interdependent and delicately balanced, if we do manage to change course, but don't get it just right, the world ends with a bang. So unless we're willing and able to take that chance, and get it just right, we're stuck pursuing our own greed down the rabbit hole, even as the ability of this planet to sustain us draws to a close.

"On the other hand robots, so far as I know, don't have the greed defect. I doubt they will adopt our constant growth model, but ironically, they can actually pull it off and they can do it, theoretically, forever. Either way, they will eventually inherit this world and beyond from us."

"So... are you saying that eventually you came to the conclusion that it is greed rather than convenience that determines the destiny of humanity?" I asked.

"They're the same thing, John. Convenience is simply greed that has become lazy and decadent," Michael answered. "And there are two additional old sayings that pertain to this subject: 'Power comes from the people,' and 'Every nation gets the government it deserves.' Our destiny, whatever it is, will be the one we deserve," he said, his features distorted by a large, silly grin.

Then he abruptly changed the subject again, "I've come to use contractions, as I'm sure you've noticed. If you don't you have to put up with constant remarks about your speech, people think there's something wrong with you and they find it very annoying. But you know, just hearing you speak makes me nostalgic for my old life," Michael said in a wistful tone. "But then I know that nostalgia is about only remembering the good parts, not the bad. And, other than Estelle, the bad did outweigh the good. I'm here to stay. But if you're convinced of your need to return to the future, it should be simple."

"Simple? How could time travel be simple? Until a few hours ago I believed that it was impossible," I said, thinking he wasn't making sense.

"Well John, I believe this comes under the heading, 'Everything is possible, some things are just more likely than others.' This has happened twice that we're aware of, once to me and once to you, so apparently, not that unlikely, in the scheme of things."

At least three times that I'm aware of, I thought, thinking of The White Rabbit and how I had followed him from 2063 to 1979. But I decided that if I interrupted him mid-thought, he might take off on another tangent, so I said nothing.

"Of course I haven't tried it myself, but I've always assumed that if I wanted to go back, all I'd have to do is reverse the process that brought me here in the first place; go back to the Garden of Eden and go back down the stairs that lead to Specs'."

"Garden of Eden, Specs'... What are you talking about?" I asked.

"The Garden of Eden is the strip club you found yourself in when you went up the stairway behind the drapes. Specs' is the bar you were drinking in on your date."

"No, I told you it was called The Rabbit Hole," I corrected him.

"Yes, they started calling it that sometime in the 21st century, but it's called Specs' in this time period."

"Well, I hope it is that simple. I guess it is worth a try. What else do I have to go on?" I considered my options, of which there seemed to be few.

"Yes, indeed, what else?" Michael said.

"So how do I get to the Garden of Eden? I have come a long way and taken a roundabout route. And I have never been this deep into North Beach, not on foot anyway. I am not sure I can find my way back," I said, realizing that I might be lost.

Michael stopped to take a drag on his pipe. He held the smoke in his lungs for a moment, then exhaled. "I don't suppose you have any 21st century pot on you, do you?" he asked. "It's so much stronger than this stuff."

"No, I do not partake. Like I said, it does not agree with me. So how do I get to the Garden of Eden?" I repeated, concerned that I was about to lose him to the drugs.

"Well... go out my door and at the bottom of the stairs turn to your right on Francisco. Then, at the bottom of the hill turn to your right again on Columbus and walk all the way to Broadway, it's like six or seven blocks. Then turn left on Broadway and it's only a couple of doors from the corner, across from the Condor Club," he said.

"So I go out here, then right, then right again, then left on Broadway," I repeated, to make sure I had it right.

"Yessss. Just stay on the hippopotamus... The hippopotamuse... Hippomoose?"

After that unintelligible sentence he fell silent and stared into space, smiling.

"Yes, well thank you for your help, Michael, but I think I should be going. I must try this out," I said, rising from my chair and starting for the door. I unlocked it and turned the handle. "Are you going to lock it behind me?" I asked. He didn't respond, so I turned to check on him, but Michael was gone.

THE HYPOTENUSE
Chapter 11

I NEARLY REACHED THE CORNER OF FRANCISCO AND COLUMBUS when I heard Michael call my name. I turned to see him hanging over the porch railing, his dress shimmering under the porch light. "Stay on the hypotenuse," he yelled to me.

"Okay, Michael, thanks," I called back to him.

"And remember, simple extrapolation isn't a reliable way to predict the future. Good luck to you, John Simon," he yelled. Then he stood upright, re-entered his apartment building and I continued on my way.

At the corner I turned right, considering his words as I did. *He is either crazy or the drugs have gotten to him,* I thought. Then it hit me; in my mind's eye I saw a rudimentary map of North Beach in which Columbus Avenue cut a diagonal across the primary grid. In doing so it formed many triangular plots of land, on all of which it was the hypotenuse. *Stay on Columbus, that's all he's saying.*

Columbus Avenue was dimly lit, which concerned me as I walked past a four story motor inn. The red brick facade of the inn contained two large openings to the ground floor parking and three small ones for human entry, plus a planter box that was recessed into the wall. These were all perfect hiding places, where I imagined a u-bee ruffian could be lying in wait for some unsuspecting person. *But you are suspecting*, I assured myself, as I stood erect and tried to appear as alert as possible.

Just beyond the inn, across Houston alley, Bimbo's 365 was still brightly lit, but nearly deserted. One car was being driven away and one man in a white smock moved at an unhurried pace.

After passing Bimbo's 365 I came to the wide intersection, where the cable car cable whirled beneath the cable car tracks. I crossed two streets, then came to a bar called La Rocca's Corner. As I passed it I was thankful for the light its large windows cast onto the street, but then I came to a dark stretch of store fronts. Toward the end of this dark stretch was a club called Dance Your Ass Off, from which emanated muted dance music. Its entryway shed light onto the street, as did the corner bar next to it.

I started to cross the next street, which was part of another wide intersection, where the street became dark again. Ahead of me on Columbus Avenue I noticed someone walking toward me in the dark. I squared my shoulders and puffed myself up, trying to look as intimidating as possible. I relaxed when I realized it was Olga from the back room of the Savoy Tivoli. She turned to my right and went to the door of a Victorian apartment building, which was on a corner that was recessed from Columbus Avenue. She stepped up to the double doors and put her key into the lock.

"Olga!" I yelled from the crosswalk, a bit more loudly than I intended to.

She started visibly, then turned to confront me. "Oh, El Futuro, it's you! You startled me," she said, placing her hand lightly on her collar bone.

"I am sorry. Is that where you live?" I asked.

"Yes, Jerry and I do. He's still at the Savoy finishing up. I came home to change because we're going to the Target Video party. We're meeting at Luther's. It's nearby, just two doors past the Postcard Palace. You can meet us there if you like. We're getting a ride from John Mutant. I'll introduce you, he has a pickup truck, so I'm sure he'd give you a ride if you don't mind riding in the bed," she offered.

"Oh thank you, Olga, I was at Luther Blue's earlier. Ivey introduced me to John and Dave Mutant as we were leaving, but I have to go home," I declined her offer.

"Well, if you change your mind, you know where Luther's is. We'll be leaving around one-thirty," she said.

"Thanks Olga. By-the-way, what time is it?" I asked, realizing it was getting late, but without my device I didn't know how late.

"It's... " she raised her arm and looked at her wrist watch. "A bit past 12:30," she reported. "Well, I have to get ready," she said, then turned her key.

"Thanks Olga," I said, as she opened her door and disappeared into the building. *Twelve-thirty, it is getting late*, I thought, and resumed my journey. The next few blocks offered little in the way of light. There were street lights, but not as bright as the ones I am used to, and few of the shops I passed were open. It seemed that if the establishment sold coffee, food or alcohol it was open at this hour, otherwise it was closed. *What a waste of city space. No wonder brick-and-mortar died.*

For the next several blocks the street became very dark and I found I was walking uphill, causing me to break out in a sweat. To occupy my mind I formulated a plan: *If I make it to The Garden of Eden, and find the stairway, and at the bottom of the stairway I find myself in The Rabbit Hole in 2063, I'm home. If I cannot find the stairwell, or if I do and find myself in Specs' in 1979, I immediately find an acceptable hotel for the night.* Somehow, having a plan made me feel better.

At Mason Street there was another wide intersection, where a cable car cable whirled beneath the cable car tracks. As I was crossing the cable car tracks, I looked to the other side of Columbus Avenue and recognized the street where I had seen a man breaking into a car. I picked up my pace, worried he might still be lurking about.

The street brightened considerably when I reached Filbert Street, where two cars were being serviced by an attendant at Tony's service station. Finally I reached the old theater Paula pointed out on our way to Luther Blue's. Its doors were open and people were exiting onto the sidewalk. With light and people all around me, I began to relax. I started to follow the sidewalk past the theater, seeing there were two open establishments ahead. The first one was named The Washington Square Bar & Grill, which made me realize that I was getting hungry. But I also realized that by walking in that direction, I was getting off of Columbus Avenue. *Stay on the hypotenuse. Stay on the hypotenuse.*

I readjusted my path, crossed Powell Street to Columbus

Avenue, then walked past a small, triangular park that was enclosed by a low iron fence. There was a bus at the curb and several passengers were boarding. I approached the corner and noticed that most of the shops at this intersection were still open. When I reached the corner, I looked diagonally across the intersection to Mario's, which made me think of food again. As I crossed Union Street the bus roared past me. I was about to cross Columbus Avenue to get something to eat, but saw that Mario's was empty except for two people who were putting the bar stools on the bar.

I was abruptly brought out of my thoughts when I bumped into a man who was coming out of a liquor store on the corner. "I am sorry," I blurted out.

"That's okay, no harm done," the man answered. I noticed he was wearing a white smock like the car attendants in front of Bimbo's 365. He slapped a pack of cigarettes against his palm several times, then opened the pack, throwing the packaging material to the ground.

"That was my fault, I was not looking where I was going. I am hungry and was looking at Mario's, but they seem to be closing," I told him.

"Oh yeah, they close at midnight," he said, removing a cigarette from his pack. "Look, I'm on break. I was working the show at Bimbo's and I was the first one they cut when business slowed down. I don't have to be over to the parking lot on Broadway until 1:30. I'm going to Sam Wo's for fried rice, you're welcome to come with. I could use some conversation before I have to go back to running cars," he offered.

"Is it close by?" I asked, feeling that I either needed to get home or find a hotel room before everything closed. The idea of sleeping in a park where people get mugged or sleeping in a doorway didn't appeal to me.

He was in the act of lighting his cigarette, so it took him a moment to respond to my question. As I waited for a response I glanced diagonally across the intersection to the dark void that was Washington Square Park. I shuddered at the prospect of sleeping in there.

He exhaled a cloud of smoke, then replied, "Yeah man, it's over in Chinatown, just off Grant. It's like a five minute walk from here," he assured me. "My name's Bill," he said, holding out his hand.

"Mine is John, John Simon," I said, shaking his hand. "Sure, I will go," I agreed, my hunger getting the better of me.

As we walked he told me about his job working for The Flying Dutchman and living in downtown San Francisco. I decided to avoid telling him I was from the future, as I was a bit leery of that after the scolding I received from DeDe. Instead I told him I was visiting from Albany across the bay. I grew up there, so I knew something about that small town, at least as it is in the 21st century. I was relieved when he told me that he had moved to San Francisco from Iowa the previous winter and had never even heard of Albany, California.

At the corner of Broadway and Columbus we stopped for the pedestrian light in front of El Cid. *Stay on the hypotenuse. Well, he did say to turn left at Broadway, so I've stayed on the hypotenuse for as long as he said I should.* I was tempted to take leave of my new acquaintance and head straight for Garden of Eden, but figured that would be rude. Besides, I was famished. Thoughts of food overcame my desire to return to the future, at least for the duration of a meal. We crossed Broadway where Grant Avenue came up from Chinatown.

We walked three blocks past closed Chinese shops, then Bill said, "It's right here." We turned to our right on Washington Street and walked to the first store front, which had a back lit plastic sign above the door that read, Sam Wo Restaurant. Below that was a much older neon sign, written in Chinese characters with a list of their specials written in English.

We entered a small, narrow room that was crowded, not with diners, but with cooks. "This place is a trip," Bill said over his shoulder, as he led me through the kitchen, where the cooks toiled over hot stoves. Midway through the kitchen we came to a podium with a cash register on it. Behind it stood a female cashier, who paid us no attention. Next to the podium were stairs that we proceeded to climb.

The second floor was filled with diners, so we climbed to the third floor, which was only half full. We entered a small, narrow dining room that had a work station on the left. The station contained an assortment of things such as coffee pots, condiments, cleaning rags, etc. As we passed the work station Bill pointed out some sort of chute in the wall. "The dumbwaiter," he commented. We sat across from one another at a table adjacent to the dumbwaiter. On the table were a salt and pepper set, a bottle of some sort of condiment and an ashtray.

A moment later a waiter walked up and tossed two menus on the table between us. "I be right back," he said, in accented English.

Bill glanced at his menu, quickly put it down, butted out his cigarette in the ashtray, then lit another. I picked up my menu to look at the offerings. Soon the waiter returned holding a scratch pad in one hand and a pencil in the other. He looked at Bill. "I know you. You come here many time. Ham flied lice," he said, then made a notation on his pad.

Bill snickered. "Yeah, but give me two orders Edsel, one of them to go," he amended his order.

"Oh boy, you hungry," the waiter said, then he looked at me.

I hesitated for a moment, then asked, "Did you say 'flied lice?'"

"Yes," the waiter replied. "I say that for white people. They think it funny. You see your friend laugh."

I was slightly confused and didn't get the joke, so I just placed my order, "I will have the chicken dumplings with rice."

I was surprised to hear him reply, "No. You don't know what you want. I know. I will bring it to you," he said, making a notation on his pad. Then he abruptly turned, walked to the stairway and disappeared into it.

I gave Bill a questioning look. "That's Edsel Fung. He's famous for being the rudest waiter in Frisco," was the explanation he gave.

While I waited for my food, I looked at my surroundings. At first the walls appeared to be wood paneled, but then I noticed that the faux wood grain was worn down in places to plain, white formica, or something equally old fashioned and cheap. Above our table a black, plastic number *3* was adhered to the wall. The lighting was bare light bulbs screwed into sockets on the wall.

They could use one of those globe light fixtures from the Savoy Tivoli.

"What do you think of this place, John? I love bringing people here for the first time. Isn't it a trip?" Bill asked.

"Yes, it has... character," I answered thoughtfully.

"John, and don't take this the wrong way, but I've noticed you speak in an unusual way."

"You mean I do not use contractions," I guessed.

"Yes! That's it. I couldn't put my finger on it, but that's exactly it. Why is that?" Bill asked.

"Well, that is how my mother raised me. And you know, Albany, California is a strange place. No one ever noticed it until I started coming to The City on the weekends," I took a chance he would believe that explanation.

I was relieved to hear him say, "Huh, I got to see this Albany, California someday. Where do you go when you come over here?" he asked.

"Oh, a lot of places, The Savoy Tivoli, Vesuvio, Enrico's, Mabuhay Gardens... "

"What's The Mab like? I've always wondered, I see these strange people waiting in line there," Bill pressed me for details.

"Well, it is strange, really loud," I struggled to describe the Mabuhay. Then I remembered Ivey's calendar that was in the breast pocket of my jacket. *If I make it back to 2063 tonight it wouldn't be good to get caught with that on me.* "Here," I said, pulling the sheet of paper from my pocket. "A woman I met there gave me this, it is a punk event calendar for next month," I said, as I handed him the calendar.

"Thanks. Sure you don't want it?" He asked, as he unfolded it.

"No, I do not think I will be around in June. Oh, and take this as well," I said, handing him Ruben's postcard.

"Thanks, so where you going after this?"

"A place called Garden of Eden," I answered.

"Me too," Bill said. "My girlfriend works there, I'm bringing her dinner. She knows I always eat here and she asked me to bring her dinner before I go back to work at the Broadway lot," he explained, as he refolded Ivey's calendar, then put it and the postcard into his hip pocket.

"Well, with you as my guide, I will not get lost," I said.

Edsel returned, reached into the dumbwaiter and pulled out a tray with our food on it. He placed two plates of food, two steel tea pots, two tea cups and a small, folded white cardboard container with a wire handle on our table. Then he wrote something on his scratch pad, tore off the sheet he wrote on and put it on our table. "You pay downstairs," he said.

"Edsel, what is the name of this dish you brought me?" I asked.

"What your name?" He asked me in return.

"John, John Simon," I answered, flattered that the rudest waiter in San Francisco seemed to be warming up to me. I held out my hand for him to shake.

"Dish called, 'John-John Simon,'" he said, then walked away and descended the stairs, his laughter filling the stairwell.

"I told you he was the rudest waiter in Frisco," Bill smiled.

I lowered my outstretched hand and picked up the scrap of paper. I looked at it and saw that the number *3* was written at the top and circled. At the bottom *$5.24* was written and circled. The rest of it was undecipherable squiggles.

Confused, I put the scrap of paper back on the table and turned it toward Bill. "This could not be right. Is this the whole bill?"

He looked at it, then answered, "Yeah, that's it. This place is cheap, isn't it?"

"It is almost free," I answered. "You have to let me pay, I insist."

"Okay by me," Bill said with a smile, then he butted out his cigarette and dug into his plate of food.

I looked at my plate, which consisted of rice and noodles that were stir fried with pieces of chicken, onion, mushrooms and some sort of greens. I took a bite. It was fairly good, but hunger probably made it taste better than it was. I looked at Bill's plate as he scooped it down. It looked similar to mine, except that there were no noodles and instead of chicken there were small, pink flecks of ham that glistened with a slight green iridescence. He didn't seem to mind, so I said nothing and concerned myself with eating as quickly as possible. When I finished I looked at the clock on the wall. It read, *1:23*.

THE GARDEN OF EDEN
Chapter 12

WE DESCENDED THE STAIRS, STOPPING AT THE CASHIER'S podium where I paid with a ten dollar bill. "Keep the change," I said with flair, and we exited Sam Wo.

Once outside, Bill stopped to light another cigarette. After exhaling he said, "I don't have much time to smoke while I'm running cars, so when I get the chance, I suck 'em down."

As we walked it occurred to me that I hadn't solved the mystery of live worms yet. "So Bill, do people in San Francisco fish in the bay?" I asked him.

"Yeah, I see them going down to the bay with fishing gear all the time, poles, crab nets, you name it. Hell, North Beach was built by fishermen," was his reply.

"So that place Figoni Hardware on Grant sells live worms as bait, I suppose."

"I'm not familiar with the place, but if they sell live worms, they're for bait. Why do you ask? Do you fish?" Bill asked.

"No. Just wondering," I replied, and congratulated myself for solving the other mystery of the night.

After a short walk we arrived at the Garden of Eden. It didn't look familiar, but since the only time I was there I was chasing The White Rabbit out of the door, I never saw the entrance.

Pacing the sidewalk in front was an older man with a trimmed, gray mustache, dressed in a suit and wearing a red fez.

"Hey George," Bill greeted him. "This is John, he's cool." George waved us through and we entered a room with too much red for my taste. Most of the walls were covered in red drapes, and the ones that weren't were painted red.

"John," Bill held out his hand, "It was good meeting you.

Oh, and thanks for dinner. Drop by the Broadway parking lot across the street next time you cross the bay to Frisco," he said, as we shook hands. "I got to go find Emilie and give her her dinner," he held up the little, white cardboard container by the wire handle. "Then I have to go back to work, I'm already running late. Have fun," he said, and wandered away looking for his girlfriend.

I walked a little further into the club, turning down several offers of drinks from half naked women on my way. I stopped and turned to get my bearings. The room looked pretty much as I remembered when I came out of the stairwell. I turned back to the wall and put out my hand. There was solid wall behind the drapes. My heart sank. Frantically I tried another spot. Then another. Finally the drapes gave way. I brushed them aside and stepped through into a dark stairwell. I felt around until I located the handrail, then hurriedly descended the stairs. In my haste I misstepped and took a tumble in the dark. Perhaps due to an adrenalin rush, I felt as though I was falling in slow motion. And then I hit my head.

♦♦♦

"John. John." Someone was repeating my name.

I opened my eyes. I was lying on my back in the hallway of The Rabbit Hole, with The White Rabbit standing over me.

"John. John, are you okay?" he asked.

"Yes, I think so," I answered, slowly sitting up and rubbing my forehead. After The White Rabbit helped me to my feet, I stood there for a moment as my head cleared.

"You got a nasty bump on the forehead. I'd put a cold compress on that, if I were you. Here you go," The White Rabbit said, holding out my device. "Thanks for letting me borrow it, my sister's going to be okay. I think the sound of my voice really picked up her spirits, so thanks again."

"My pleasure," I said, as I took my device from him.

"Got to go," he said, then left me standing in the hallway wondering what just happened.

I slid my device into my pocket, and then it occurred to me that my bank card might still be in the ATM. I entered the barroom and began walking toward the front of the room. I was surprised to see Sarah still sitting at our table and that the ice in my drink hadn't melted. Sarah was looking at her device, which cast an even blue tone on her face. "Sarah," I greeted her hesitantly.

"Johnny Boy!" Sarah said, looking up from her device, causing her face to change from an even blue tone to an eerie under lit blue.

"Sarah, I..."

"Did you get your device back?"

"Yes I did," I answered, wondering why she didn't ask me where I had been. "It is right here," I said, pulling it out and activating it. I had it set to open to the clock face and I saw that it was only 8:24. I looked out the front door and it was still twilight.

"Did you bump your head? There's a red knot on your forehead," Sarah said.

"Yes. I think so," I replied.

"Are you okay?" She seemed concerned.

"Yes, I am fine. But I think I left my bank card in the ATM."

"So... you better go check," she said.

"Yes, I will be right back." Before I reached the ATM I could see my bank card protruding from the slot. I pulled it out, put it into my pocket, then returned to Sarah.

"Do you want to get another drink here, or go somewhere else?" she asked.

"I think I have had enough of this place for one night," I replied.

Sarah took a last sip of her drink, then stood. "Do you want to go home?" she asked.

"No, I am fine. We can go to another place for a drink," I replied, not wanting to put a damper on our first in person date.

As we walked toward the door, Hatter turned from a conversation he was having at the bar. "John, did you find him?" he asked.

"Yes," I replied. "He was in the restroom just like you said."

"Oh good. And you got your device back?" he asked.

"Yes," I pulled it out of my pocket to illustrate, then put it back.

"Good. All's well that ends well," he said, then turned back to his conversation.

"Hey, big spender, thanks for the tip," the bartender said loudly and sarcastically, while looking at me. I didn't understand what he was talking about, but figured it was time for me to leave.

We walked through the door, Sarah took me by the arm and we started walking out of the alley. Before we reached the sidewalk on Columbus Avenue we were confronted by two men in uniforms. Both had patches on their chest that read, Office of the Seer. "Are you John Simon?" one of them asked, giving me a stern look.

"Yes," I responded, as Sarah let go of my arm.

"Let me see your device," he demanded.

"Should I activate it?" I asked, as I pulled it from my pocket.

"No need to," was his reply. He took my device and linked it to a device attached to his belt. My device came to life and he began scrolling through my files.

"Do you need my bank card," I asked, trying to be cooperative.

"That won't be necessary," he replied without looking up.

"What is this all about?" Sarah asked.

The man with my device stopped for a moment, looked at her and asked her her name.

"Sarah Peterson," she answered in a defiant tone. "I think we are owed an explanation. I am a twenty-five percenter, you know. I work at the Uni-Gon in Cupertino."

"It is okay, Sarah. I am sure he will find this is a mistake. Let the man do his job," I said, worried she would get us into trouble.

The man went back to scrolling through my files. "Okay, Mr. Simon, you are going to have to come with us," he said. "There is someone who wants to See you. And, yes, that is with a capital *S*."

I was shocked. "But why? What have I done?"

"I am sure you know what you have done," was his reply.

"Sir, this must be a mistake," Sarah said. "I have been with John all evening. We ate dinner and had a couple of drinks, that is all."

"Ms. Peterson, this is official business—stay out of it, unless you want to jeopardize your own position."

The second man, who had been silent up to this point, said, "Come on." He took me firmly by the arm and I was escorted out of the alley.

"John, I will see that this is cleared up," Sarah said to my back, "We will go out for drinks again tomorrow night, I promise you."

Office of the Seer

THE SEER
Chapter 13

THAT WAS THE LAST I SAW OF SARAH. THEY BROUGHT ME HERE and put me in this room. I sat here waiting for what must have been two hours, not knowing what I was being held for. Finally I heard a disembodied female voice say my name.

"Yes," I answered, a bit startled.

"You will address me as Seer during our brief encounter," she instructed me.

The voice seemed to be coming from above. "Where are you, Seer?" I asked.

"You have no need to see me," she said, in a slightly annoyed tone of voice. "I will do the Seeing. Do you know why you are here?"

"No, Seer, I do not know why I am here. I think it is a mistake." I answered.

"It is no mistake, John Simon. We both know why you are here, do we not?" she said.

Other than Michael, I had never met a Seer. Since she said "we both know," I felt I had little choice in what to answer, otherwise I would be questioning her knowledge, exactly what Michael had warned against. "Yes, Seer, I know why I am here," I answered.

"Very good, John Simon. You have already made progress." After giving me that positive reinforcement she gave me my instructions, "The rest is easy, you simply have to write a confession of your crimes and then you will be free to go. However, it may take you a while to write it, so I have arranged for these accommodations for you. This room is not convenient, but your needs will be met. You will be fed three times a day, via the dumbwaiter you see on the wall. With your first meal you will also receive an envelope containing a pad of writing paper and pencils. You do know how to write by hand, do you not, John Simon?"

"Yes, Seer. But I have not done so since grade school, I swear... "

"Good," she cut my sentence short. "While you are here, writing by hand is authorized. Actually, it is demanded. When your pencils need sharpening, put them on your food tray when you are finished eating. If you run out of paper, put the empty pad of paper on the tray. The next time you are fed you will receive sharpened pencils and paper as you need them."

"But Seer... " I objected, unclear what form my confession should take.

She cut me off again, "There are no buts here, John Simon, only positive results. You have all of the information you need. The sooner you finish your project, the sooner you can return to your convenient life. Is that clear?"

"Yes, Seer," I replied, seeing no wisdom in questioning her further.

"Good day to you, John Simon," she said, then fell silent.

That was the only interaction I had with her. I have been in this room ever since. On occasion a disembodied voice, usually male, has spoken to me. Nothing interesting, just things like, "Time to put your food tray back in the dumbwaiter," "time to clean your room," things like that. And he always refers to me as J6, not by my name. That is the only human contact I have had since I have been here.

You see those happy faces on the wall back there? That is how I keep track of time, after every third meal I draw one on the wall with one of my pencils. If I did not do that I would lose track of time. I counted them again a few days ago and I believe I have been here for over six months. Well, I must continue my writing, I think I am almost done.

EPILOGUE

CONVENIENT CONVE
CONVENIENT CONV
CONVENIENT CONV
t CONVENIENT CONV
T CONVENIENT CON
T CONVENIENT CON
ST CONVENIENT CO
NT CONVENIENT CO
NT CONVENIENT CC
ENT CONVENIENT C
NT CONVENIENT C
NT CONVENIENT C
ENT CONVENIENT
IENT CONVENIENT
IENT CONVENIENT
IENT CONVENIENT

THE DETENTION CENTER

TWO GUARDS CAME DOWN THE HIGHLY POLISHED, linoleum tile corridor. They both wore dark blue uniforms with patches sewn on above their left breast pockets. The patches were oval with Security embroidered in a curve along the top and Detention Center embroidered along the bottom. One of the guards had the number 1089 embroidered in large type in the middle of his patch. The other guard had 1136 embroidered on his. 1136 also wore a polished, brass badge that read, Trainee. They walked on opposite sides of the brightly lit hallway, stopping briefly to look at the small video displays mounted on the doors that lined it.

1136 lingered for a moment at the door marked D3. "Hey 1089, D3's chatty today. Who's she talking to?"

1089 crossed the hallway and looked at the display. He reached up and adjusted two knobs, magnifying the area where D3 had written on the wall with a pencil. He shrugged and said, "No one. Herself. The walls. Who knows? Have you noticed that she writes the word 'convenient' on the wall after every third meal? She's been doing that for months. She's probably about done, and she's been a hard nut to crack. Which reminds me, they'll be feeding her soon," 1089 replied.

"Again? Wasn't she just fed a couple hours ago?"

"Yeah, but she's been here nearly four months," 1089 mentioned over his shoulder as he crossed back to the other side of the hallway. "We slowly change their feeding schedule the longer they're here." 1089 explained, then waited for 1136 to ask the obvious question.

"Why?"

"Look 36, the reason they're here is to be broken. You see, inevitably they find a way to mark the passing of time. It always includes counting their meals, that's pretty much the only thing that punctuates their day. We see to that. At first we feed them three meals a day, at normal intervals, with a long break between dinner and breakfast to simulate night. Once they start marking time we slowly shorten the night break and the intervals between meals, decrease the portion size and increase the number of meals per day. Today D3's scheduled for six meals, almost evenly spaced. In her mind today will count for two days. Most detainees only last about two months. Very few make it past four."

"Why does she write 'convenient'?"

1089 shrugged again, pushing out his lower lip, "Who knows, 36? Some people write their name. There's a guy upstairs in J6 that came in a few days before Miss D3. He draws a happy face. Most just put a hash mark. The point is, they mark time and we control the flow of time, so far as they're concerned."

"What happens after she breaks, 1089?"

"Realignment. They'll take her from this cell and put her in the Psychological Realignment Center. That usually only takes about two weeks."

"And then?" 1136 asked.

"Then she'll be cycled back into a job. Not her old job, that risks screwing up the realignment. But it will be a job of the same type."

"Won't she have to be retrained?"

"No, not extensively. The Realignment Center's methods are very convenient. They can pick and choose what to remove and what to leave behind," 1089 explained.

"Huh. Pretty depressing, isn't it?"

"I'm used to it, 36. I've worked in Detention for eight years. You're just beginning. You'll get used to it."

"Maybe. Well, I'm going off shift. See you tomorrow?" 1136 asked.

"No, I'm off the next couple days. See you Wednesday."

1136 walked away and a female guard appeared. Her patch read 1095. "Hey 89, how have you been?" she asked.

"I'm good, 95. You?"

"No complaints. So how's 36 working out?"

"He's coming along. He's still asking awkward questions, but that's understandable, he's just beginning his training. If he's still asking questions like that in a month that could be a problem. But for now he's progressing normally," 1089 answered.

"You get off soon, don't you?"

"Yes I do, 95," 1089 raised his arm to check his watch. "In twenty minutes."

"Me too. Want to get a drink after work?"

"Sure, it's my Friday," 1089 answered, relishing his approaching weekend.

1095 lowered her voice, "Oh, 89, let's go somewhere inconvenient," she suggested, stressing the first syllable of her last word.

1089 looked around quickly, then whispered his response, "Ever been to The Rabbit Hole?"

The Photographer

A LARGE MAN STOOD SWEATING IN A DARKROOM, BATHED IN red light. The darkroom was part of the ASUC studios which were located in the basement of the ASUC building, on the University of California, Berkeley campus. He had just finished developing numerous rolls of film that he shot the night before. He carefully hung them to dry on a wire that was strung behind the photo developing sink, between opposing walls. He went to the wall near the door and switched the white light on, then went back to the film strips that hung like clothes drying on a line. He began looking at them to get an idea of what he had captured on film the previous night.

"Good one of Mark the doorman," he commented to the empty room. "Great shots of Holly, what a little beauty." Holding it carefully by the edges he repositioned the film strip to see it better. "What? One of the speakers at the Mab? Why would I photograph that? And here's another of the same speaker... He! He! He!" he giggled in a high pitched tone. "What was I thinking?" At that point he let the film strip drop to hang from the wire. "I need to take a break," he said, then opened the door of the darkroom and walked out into the lobby.

As he walked through the lobby of the ASUC studios he stopped to speak with the woman who ran the facility. "Helen, do you know if Ruben's working at Berkeley Arts today?"

"Oh, hi Hugh. It's Sunday, so I think he is," she replied. "I know he's coming in on Tuesday to do a run of color Xerox prints. And I think Tuesday is his birthday."

"Well, it's just over on Durant, I'll go by and check. If he is working, he should be getting off for lunch soon. I feel like a Top Dog hot link, then maybe some beer and a little Missile Command at the Dew Drop Inn," he said, and the jovial, bespectacled photographer walked out of the door and into a warm, spring afternoon.

This book is set in Adobe Garamond Pro. Most of the images were produced with Affinity Designer, though a few were done in Adobe Illustrator. This book was a transition period, from Adobe to Affinity software, for the graphics department of Fast, Cheap & Easy Graphics. The photos were also handled in Affinity Photo and the book layout was done with Affinity Publisher.

Made in the USA
Middletown, DE
28 February 2022

61902875R00110